JEAN HARLOW AND THE LEGEND OF STONEFISH CREEK

By

Jes McCutchen

Jean Harlow and the Legend of Stonefish Creek
By Jes McCutchen

MANUSTRIUM
MEDIA

Manustrium Media
848 S Indianapolis Ave
Tulsa OK 74112

Cover Illustration | Ezra Blank
Cover Design | Maxi Vittor
Editor | Jeni Chappelle
Editor | Racheal Daodu

Library of Congress Control Number | 2024912871
ISBN: *(ebook)* | 979-8-9859486-5-3
ISBN: *(Print Edition)* | 979-8-9859486-4-6

While a work of fiction, there may be a handful of recognizable places such as those someone from Oklahoma has perhaps visited in their youth as part of a field trip. All the people and places are works of fiction in this work of fiction.

Also by Jes McCutchen

Chronicles of My Alien Invasion Life
A Mean Piece of Water
Between the Mess and Magic (editor)

With Horns and Rattles Press
Fish Gather to Listen (editor)
Bitter Become the Fields (editor)

Content Warnings:

Please take care of yourself, and reach out to me on social media or via email jesmccutchen@gmail.com if you have any questions or would like more details about the CWs.

- ☞ Panic Attacks
- ☞ Anxiety
- ☞ Possession
- ☞ Blood
- ☞ Drowning
- ☞ Animal Death (not a pet!)
- ☞ Vomit

988 is the US national mental health crisis and suicide prevention hot-line. Take care of you and yours, friends.

To Jean Carol Bacon Dix, all the Jeans that follow her, and all of those Jeans' siblings. May a sibling or a cousin always have your back.

You're wearing a backpack. You can tell because your hands grip the straps.
The nails are painted but chipped.
There is a crowd of humans around you. It is loud. They all seem excited.
Looking left, there is a long hallway.
Looking right, there is another similar hallway.
The lights are bright and unnatural.
A bell rings and everyone scatters.
You follow some of them. Your feet know which way to go.

Chapter 1

"Hello? Earth to Jean."

"What?" I spun around and realized Byron was walking alongside me. "Oh, hi."

He nudged my shoulder. "You're not going to get called on to recite a chapter of the book in front of the class, so you can stop that train of thought if you'd like."

I let out a breath I hadn't meant to be holding. "Is there, like, a sign that lights up above my head when I'm in a loop?"

Laughing, he draped an arm around my shoulders as we walked into our last period for the day. "Nope, I just speak Jean fluently."

I hooked my backpack on the plastic chair and slid into my seat at exactly the farthest left and one seat behind the front row of the class. Byron took a desk next to me.

"I'll have you know I was not thinking of getting called on."

"Oh, really?" He raised an eyebrow at me and pulled out his spiral notebook and a mechanical pencil, clicking it a few times before I handed him extra lead.

"I was thinking about what I would need to do if an airplane crashed in the neighborhood." Which was the truth and Byron was one of the only people I would consider voicing my intrusive thoughts aloud to. He'd heard worse.

Byron shook his head slightly, mop of curls bouncing across his forehead. "You are so weird, Jean." Then he booped me on the nose and chuckled. "Thanks for being my friend."

"Ugh, don't be such a dork." But it worked, and the knot of anxiety in my chest loosened.

Just as the bell rang, Frankie slipped into her seat across the room and stuck her tongue out at me with an impish smile like she'd done every single time we had a class together.

Even though I'm the younger sister by a year, we've been in the same grade since second because Frankie got super sick for a really long time and our parents decided it would be less stressful for her to just go ahead and repeat a grade. But they wanted us to make our own friends and stuff, so throughout elementary school we were in separate classes.

She gave me a mock frown when I didn't reciprocate, just like I haven't every single time since that first class together in sixth grade.

Luckily, she was just as big of a nerd as I was, and despite her deviant line-toeing with the always nearly being tardy shenanigans, she would never be late or cut up during class unless it was truly warranted.

By mutual understanding, we've sat apart from the beginning, knowing full well we'd get each other in trouble if we sat together. I prefer classes with Frankie. We're a good foil to each other on subjects. Ones she excels at, I'm crap in and vice versa, which made studying and projects easier.

The day passed very much like every other first day of school, and because I was keen on getting everything organized ahead of time when I could, we'd already been to the open house and schedule pickup so even the new day one information was actually two weeks old for me and my friends.

I did not know how any of my friends were going to make it in the real world without me dragging them to every organizational opportunity after we graduated.

Our last class went about like the others. The teacher went over the class syllabus for the semester, rules about when we can get up and pee, penalties for turning in work late. The usual.

At least Mr. Peterson didn't give us homework like three of my other teachers did. And he wrapped up early and let us work on other stuff so long as we kept the volume down. I managed to get two of my three assignments finished before the final bell.

When it rang, I piled my books and supplies away and met Frankie at the door.

"Walking to Stonefish?" she asked, taking off her jean jacket and slinging it over her shoulder.

"Yep, you coming, Byron?" I asked as we made our way outside and met up with two more of our friends.

"Sure," he said, "though I don't know if I'm cool enough to walk with you, Frankie."

"You're not, but I'll allow it." Frankie winked and sauntered ahead of us a bit, catching up with two more of our friends.

I glanced at Byron. "Are you blushing?"

"I don't know. Do you think she was flirting?"

"Byron, you are my best friend. And I love you dearly. But please don't let my sister break your heart."

"I make absolutely zero promises." He grinned at me and walked a little faster to join the group. Byron was pretty sure he was gay, but he'd had a soft spot for Frankie since we were little kids.

"Come on, Jean. Get those legs going a little faster," Frankie called, and I shook my head. I knew where we were all going. There was no need to hurry.

"It's too nice of a day to rush." I pulled out my camera and headphones, drowning out the chatter of my friends as we walked past the parking lot and across the empty practice fields toward Stonefish Creek Park, which we liked to cut through to get to our houses.

Oklahoma liked to be very unpredictable when it came to the weather, so pleasant, slightly breezy late summer days were something I cherished. Especially after being stuck inside all day for school.

The five of us crossed one of the long wooden bridges and headed to our spot in the sunken pavilion. Years ago, it had blown off during a tornado or windstorm, and the top landed half in and half out of the swampy part of the creek. We'd commandeered it the summer Frankie and I finally got permission to play anywhere in the boundary of the park without adult supervision. Only half the metal on the roof remained, but the structure was sturdy.

It took ages, but we scrounged enough scrap wood to make a platform inside the beams, and it's only gotten more elaborate since then. Every once in a while, another group of kids would make their own forts, but we had a solid claim staked at the pavilion. Two winters ago, we actually got enough snow for some epic group-on-group snowball fights.

The most memorable of which was when Frankie and Meara in camo makeup pelted seventh graders with dozens of snowballs from the roof of the pavilion. It had taken them hours to stock up and get everything onto the roof. It was epic.

Ahead of me, Frankie and Sam grabbed the long board and laid it across the small space between the edge of the creek and the first metal step into the fort. The space was just far enough that jumping risked spending the rest of the afternoon in soggy sneakers but short enough that just having one step on the plank was enough to get across.

The hideout wasn't top secret or anything, and it wasn't like the creek was deep, but it made it feel more ours having a few obstacles to get into it.

Balancing without using my hands, I hopped over and took my usual seat by the far wall, where I could watch the running water and the path on the far side of the swampy part.

"It really sucks that we don't have a single class together." Meara pouted and sat down next to me, pulling my hair out of its ponytail and brushing it with a comb she pulled out of her bag.

"For real. And we have so many of the same teachers too. I really thought we would have at least one." I closed my eyes and relaxed for maybe the first time in eight hours.

"At least we have lunch at the same time." She ran her fingers and the comb down, parting my hair into two big sections and giving me goosebumps.

"That's true. And we can do most of our homework together, since most of the classes are the same." A few minutes later, my hair was in two big braids that she looped like a crown around my head and pinned in place with three bobby pins. In third grade, she decided she was going to be a hairstylist, and I pinky promised her I'd let her and only her do my hair forever and always.

She had since gotten into science and pivoted on her career goals, but I was so used to her fixing my hair that I lawyered the pinky promise. Turned out, those went both ways, and she has kept doing my hair since. Which all my friends agreed was good because otherwise it would be in a permanent ponytail.

Frankie balanced on the metal frame and came to stand in front of us. "How come you never do my hair anymore, Meara?"

"Well, Frankie, you shaved your head so..." Meara wagged her comb at Frankie, whose hair was as short as it had ever been, less than a quarter of an inch all around.

"Oh yeah, that." Swinging herself onto the higher rafters, Frankie stood with her head poking out of the top of the pavilion.

"You can do my hair," Sam offered, and Meara complied, combing his thick hair until it poofed up like an anime character.

The rest of us stretched out on the planks and exchanged notes about the teachers we were stuck with for a few minutes until, from above, Frankie shushed us.

"What?" Byron called up to her.

She ducked her head inside and glared at him, her face paled. Pressing her finger to her lips, she mouthed, *Shut up*. Then she motioned for us to climb up with her.

"What's going on, Frankie?" I whispered, but she shook her head at me silently and pointed up.

Sam climbed up first, followed by the rest of us as quietly as we could.

When we were all peeking over the roof top, Frankie pointed to the south, toward the bridge we crossed to get into the park.

I tried to see what she was seeing. There was lots of wildlife in the park, but it didn't usually come out during the daytime. We'd spent plenty of hours playing Harriet the Spy though, so part of me was looking for people making out which was peak drama when we were seven-year-olds.

Frankie stared directly ahead, squinting.

"What are we looking for?" Meara whispered, glancing at the rest of us.

Shrugs all around.

"Hey, Frankie," Sam started, but she waved him off, not looking away from the spot across the water.

"There's nothing there," Byron whispered, a puzzled look on his face as he glanced between Frankie and the spot she was transfixed on.

Then a snap came from behind us, breaking the silence.

All five of us jumped, and Meara slipped from where she was standing on the metal rungs. She let out a cry and lost her footing. But Byron caught her, and Sam helped him lower her to the platform just a few feet below, missing the gap that opened to water.

Behind us, there was a rustling and another snap.

Then Sam's little brother and their seventy-five-pound retriever mix clonked out of the trees.

"Sam!" he called.

"You just scared the crap out of us, Henry," I called out, laughing.

"Holy moly." Meara laughed nervously.

"Mom says you have to walk Mojito because I have to get to karate," Henry called, holding out Mojito's leash.

"Okay, okay, I'm coming." Sam laughed too and climbed down to grab his backpack. "Well, now that I'm thoroughly jumpy, I'm outta here, y'all."

"Don't we get doggo pets first?" Meara asked and jumped down to let Mo lick her all over the face before she would let Sam take the dog.

"I should head out too. I'll see you all tomorrow." Byron laughed and climbed down. "Sam, wait up."

"Byron will do anything to spend time with that dog." Meara and I laughed. "Not that I blame him. That dog is the best one of the planet."

I started to climb down but realized Frankie was still staring at the same spot. I shook her shoulder gently. "Hey, it was just Henry and Mo."

She turned slowly and looked at me then nodded. We climbed down and decided we would all head out. The three of us made our way home. Meara lived a few houses closer to the park than us, so we waved as she peeled off.

As we walked up our front steps, though, Frankie turned to me. "That's not what I felt."

Chapter 2

"Come on, Frankie," I called from the downstairs. "We're going to be late."

It was back to school club night. I was in charge of the information table for the Students for the Protection of the Environment, and we still had setup to do. No way could I trust Blakely and Jack to take care of it all themselves, even if they were technically higher-ranking officers.

Frankie and Byron were working their own table at the event, so it wasn't like I was the only one who needed to get there. I was just the only one who wanted to get there *on time*.

And by "on time," I meant thirty minutes early. If you're not ten minutes early you're five minutes late, which was something I liked to say but my therapist absolutely railed against.

"One second," Frankie called from our room. "Lucifer hasn't come inside yet."

"She's a half-outside cat, Frankie. Luce will be fine," I hollered back. I knew Frankie was going to leave the window open anyway, so Lucifer would just be able to get right back out when she wanted.

Our moms were both in the living room watching the news.

"Your sister is getting anxious," Mom called up.

"My sister is always anxious." Frankie took the stairs down three at a time and landed with a hop in the foyer, planting a cheerful kiss on my cheek.

"Is that what you're wearing?" I looked Frankie's coveralls up and down. "We're supposed to do club stuff."

"What? I have my shirt on." She winked, unzipping the jumpsuit and letting last year's creative writing club T-shirt peek out just a smidge.

"That's like wearing green underwear on Saint Patrick's Day and telling people they're not allowed to pinch you." I was decked out in last year's hand-printed shirts we'd done with the art club and my matching reusable tote bag. We'd all thrifted or just shopped our closets for the shirts, and someone in the art club helped us make a screen so we could make them ourselves at school.

I was also wearing a matching bandana.

I was maybe possibly slightly going too far with the merch.

As though reading my mind, Frankie laughed. "You look fine, Jean. Very environmental."

"Bye folks," I called as we walked outside to meet up with the others.

"See you all later but not too late," Ma called after us, getting a thumbs-up from Frankie and finger guns from me.

We were a very normal and not at all dorky family.

When we got to Byron's house, he was waiting for us outside with Sam, so we were going to be on time after all.

And by on time, I meant ten minutes early as a sacrifice for my friends. Because in Jean's super fun anxiety brain, on time was five minutes late. Did I mention that already? I feel like maybe I did.

The first couple days of school had gone well. My classes were working out how I'd expected them to. I had a handful of Advanced Placement courses that were going to be tricky, but manageable. And I'd taken my parent's advice and dropped one of them so I could have more fun working on the yearbook staff and with my other clubs.

Though stressing out about equally representing everyone in the senior class in the yearbook photos was not what I would call fun. At the end of last year when we had wrapped up the final pages, I ran into someone I'd never seen in the bathroom washing her hands, and it dawned on me that, if I'd never seen her, that meant she wasn't in the yearbook.

I had a bit of a meltdown and maybe cried on her a bit before she figured out what I was upset about and let me know she was actually the daughter of one of the teachers just visiting from out of state.

But still.

Between being assistant photo editor and also secretary and treasurer of the environmental club, I was going to have plenty to keep me busy and put on my college applications. Frankie could have run for offices in lots of clubs, but she stuck with creative writing exclusively. I was worried she might be missing out, but she came to so many events with me, she was practically in those clubs too.

We chose tables relatively close together in the cafeteria and spent the next hour and a half explaining, mostly to first years, the club options. A handful of them came with their parents, and you could tell that they were regretting it, based on the many bashful looks they cast around the room once they realized that not everyone had a chaperone.

Everyone wanted more people than the previous year to join their clubs, though a few transfers came as well. Plus the kids who realized kinda last minute that being in clubs was good to put on resumes of all types, not just for college.

I spent some time taking a few photos for the yearbook on the digital camera that I had on loan for this and a few more back-to-school events over the course of the week.

Then, using real film in the SLR camera I'd gotten repaired at the small camera shop downtown, I took a shot of Byron and Frankie poring over something one of them had written, heads bent together and focused.

Both of them were fantastic writers, but I was obviously biased, which both would jump to tell anyone I was talking to about it.

Truly though, my friends are so talented.

At the click of the camera, Frankie looked up and stuck her tongue out at me, just quickly enough that I was sure the next shot I took would be a blurry grin from her.

I'd been asking my moms for my own darkroom for forever, but we "didn't have any place to put it," which was true and annoying. Luckily for me, one of the perks of being on the yearbook staff was that I got access to the old photo lab.

I'd spent a large chunk of the summer doing research on how to get it working, and Mrs. Camp even let me come by to clean it up a few times. I still had to make room for the computers and digital camera equipment, but over the last couple weeks of school, I'd gotten the photo lab almost functional.

Fingers crossed, this roll of film would be my first developed old school and by me.

Things at the event were winding down when someone I didn't recognize came over.

"Hi, so, what do you all do?"

I stood up, my foot catching gracefully on the chair and knocking it almost over, but the stranger caught it before it hit the floor. Unfortunately, I'd already flinched quite dramatically at the anticipated clatter.

"Sorry, you okay?" She helped me steady myself as I unwrapped my legs from their metal chair leg snare.

"Yeah, yes, yeah, I'm fine." I straightened up and sighed. "Just. Clumsy. Sometimes."

She chuckled. "Those cafeteria chairs have it out for us, I think."

I nodded in agreement. "For real. Why do the legs stick out so far? But only in the front? The design makes no sense."

"I bet the school got them for a really good deal or someone knows someone in the big chair business. Anyone with a bigger budget wouldn't use these."

"Hopefully, they put all the money they saved cutting chair corners toward, like, books or something useful," I offered.

"Or medical equipment, you know, for all the chair casualties." She grinned.

I liked this person.

"Hi, I'm Jean, she/her pronouns." I stuck out my hand, and she took it in hers.

"Lyla, she/her. So, you're in charge of the environment?"

I couldn't help laughing. "I mean, no. We wouldn't need this club if I was."

"You'd just burn it all down?" she asked conspiratorially.

"Something like that." I chuckled. "But no, I'm just one of the officers. Blakely is in charge, but she's not here tonight. Some sort of sports ball thing going on."

"Well then, Jean, I guess I'll get the pitch from you. Why should I join your illustrious club?" Lyla crossed her arms and put on a seriously discerning face, one hand on her chin thoughtfully.

"First off, you get to spend a lot of time picking up rivers, and sometimes we find really weird stuff."

"What sort of weird stuff?" She leaned forward, her curiosity obviously piqued.

"Like, once we found a complete opossum skeleton. Like, the entire thing."

"Did you touch it?" she asked with a frown that felt more interested than put off.

"I kinda just poked it with a stick, then I took a picture." Why was I telling this cute girl all of this? Like, the nerd was just spewing out of me.

"Eww, you are really weird, Jean, steward of the environment." But she said it in a kind way, and I thought maybe she was flirting with me a little.

"Take a flier and come to our first big cleanup this weekend. You can also earn service hours if you need any."

"Do I look like someone who does crime?" She gasped and held her hand dramatically to her chest. "Or worse, like a National Honor Society nerd?"

"I'm going to say you're right in the center of that Venn diagram," I teased. Wait, was I flirting back?

"I will see you there, then." Lyla took the flier and tucked it into the pocket of her jacket and sauntered off to another table, making a dramatic move of steering clear of the chairs.

"Who was that?" Frankie asked, stepping over from her table to mine and watching Lyla's back.

"Lyla," I responded, feeling my face warm and stacking the fliers in a neat pile, which they were already in.

"Is she new?" Frankie knew I was queer, but she didn't usually catch me flirting with people.

"I don't know. It didn't come up." I realized I hadn't asked her anything about herself other than her name.

"I don't recognize her." Frankie said it in a way that felt overly curious.

"Neither do I. She's probably a transfer. Moved here or something."

"Think she might want to join creative writing club?"

"I have absolutely no idea." I shrugged. "But I can try and find out for you." Literally any excuse to talk to her again.

Lyla looked back at me from the Pep Club table and gave me a smile and a small wave from across the room.

I couldn't help the grin spreading on my face as I waved back.

"You should get her number, sis." Frankie elbowed me and pulled teasingly at one of my braids.

Chapter 3

"Bless you, my child." Byron bowed dramatically as I handed him a steaming cup of coffee from the thermos at the back of the truck. I found it was worth the budget expenditure to go for donuts and coffee to kick off these river cleanup projects.

I'd done the math. Attendance went up 35 percent when I promised hot beverages, even if it was already steamy outside. I also had coolers of ice water that anyone could refill their bottles with.

"Saved you a chocolate glazed," Frankie said, holding out the donut and a napkin.

"And blessings to you as well, my other child." Byron took the treat and shoved half of it in his mouth in one bite.

"Y'all are so weird." Meara took a bite of her own donut, tossing the napkin into one of the garbage bags.

Sam was also there, his best doggo Mojito in tow and wearing her little reflective vest that had patches all over it that said cute things about being an adventure dog who loved pets. Seriously, the best dog.

Along with Blakely and Jack, the other officers for the club, there were about a dozen other high schoolers, most of whom I recognized.

Blakely, the president, was going around with a clipboard for anyone who needed to get their hours as part of community service requirements. We had two sponsors with us, but they were in a separate group with other adults and mostly left us to run it on our own.

It was really great seeing how much the water cleanups had grown over the years. This time, we were focusing on the culverts that drained into the creek and pond waterways that led into Stonefish Creek Nature Park.

I always started the year out with a cleanup project close to the school. It made the logistics of getting everyone to the right place much simpler.

A few minutes later, once Blakely had gotten everyone signed in, I hopped up onto the bed of my truck, and everyone gathered around. Speaking in front of a group at school in a class was always so much stress. But when I was outside, doing something that meant so much to me, it was like my body belonged to a whole other person.

Frankie was constantly suggesting I become a park ranger so I could live with so much less anxiety, and I didn't disagree with that idea.

"Okay, everyone, I'm going to do a rundown on safety." I had the speech down to a science. Like a flight attendant telling people about what to do with an oxygen mask. "Wear gloves, even if you don't mind getting dirty. That's going to happen anyway. This is to keep you from getting cut."

Jack walked through the crowd, handing out gloves to everyone who needed a pair. A few of us had our own, knowing the one-size-fits-all sets did not, in fact, fit all.

"Stay in at least pairs. Everyone should have a buddy," I said. Meara and Frankie made a big show of picking each other in a tackling hug that made everyone laugh. "Leave dead things. We're here for trash, not for critters."

We'd run into our fair share of dead squirrels and such, and the risk of disease made that rule important. If we ever found something bigger, like a deer, I had the number for the park manager and animal control.

"And also alive things," Jack added. "If you get bit by a raccoon, you're on your own."

"That's not true," one of the sponsors countered. "Please let us know if you get bit."

"Anyway," I said. "Walk along the side until your bags are full, then you can bring them back to the truck. We'll unload at the dumpster and recycling containers behind the school when we're finished. We'll be out here until noon, so that's plenty of time. Good luck, everyone! Go, environment!" At that point, I never really knew what to do with my hands, so I went with the old trusty finger guns and hopped down off the tailgate.

I was handing out large contractor trash bags when a grinning figure walked up, her hands in the pockets of some overalls that had obviously been used to garden and/or paint.

"Lyla, you made it." A most likely dorky grin on my face, I asked, "Do you want some coffee?"

"That sounds great," she said, taking one of the mugs from the plastic tub and filling it up. "Also, since I'm new to this and all, I was wondering if you'd maybe be my buddy. I want to learn the ropes from an expert."

"You want me to teach you how to clean up trash?" I laughed and took two contractor bags for us.

"For all you know, I'm a rich girl who's never had to even consider trash in her whole life." Lyla pulled on gloves, and the two of us walked toward the culvert, following my friends.

"I suppose that could be true and this is like a reverse Cinderella situation."

"Plus, I know you know where all the weird stuff is." She winked, actually winked, at me.

I considered slowing down our pace and maybe the two of us could just walk together the whole time, but we caught up to Byron, Meara, Sam, and Frankie, who were already stopping to pick up garbage.

"Hey, everyone," I announced, introducing Lyla to them all.

With a "this litter isn't gonna gather itself" from Frankie, we all made our way to the edge of the cement drainage. Each neighborhood in the area had some, as well as the school ditches that were put in to take care of any water runoff. Not everyone knew that the water all went into the creek and marsh in Stonefish Creek before running to the Arkansas River.

It was supposed to be just rainwater, but so much more got dumped in it. We'd been slowly adding signage letting people know, but there was only so much the five-dollar dues and annual recycled art sale fundraiser could cover.

Maybe Frankie was right. I should probably plan a career outdoors.

Most of the groups headed south, so we took the shorter way north.

"Let's get this part knocked out, and then we can head downstream," Meara suggested.

"Good idea. By the time our bags are full," Byron pointed out, "we'll be back by the truck."

The water here was almost nonexistent, and two skateboarders were using the smooth sides and the flat bottom like a half-pipe, barely getting their boards wet. They looked around ten or eleven, and I had a fleeting moment of FOMO, wondering if it was too late for me to learn how to skateboard.

Then the slightly smaller one wiped out, and the FOMO evaporated as quickly as it came. He bounced right back, but I did not think I would have.

"We haven't had rain in days," I explained as we spread out across the ditch, picking up candy wrappers and cigarette butts and the occasional beer can.

"Does it ever fill all the way up?" Lyla asked, untangling some string from a clump of branches.

"Rarely, but it gets close sometimes. During thunderstorms and things. Gotta watch out for flash floods."

She nodded, as if trying to picture it.

The six of us reached the end of the ditch, where it led to two long metal pipes.

Lyla bent down and peered into one. "What's on the other side?"

"It just leads to the other side of the road. There's drainage over there too," Meara said.

"Oh cool. Like a tunnel under the road?"

"Well, no. There's not a big opening like on this side," Sam clarified.

"Have you been through it?" Lyla asked, crouching by the opening.

"Of course." Frankie looked down the other one.

"Not me. I'm claustrophobic," Byron said.

"Me too, plus it's soggy in there," Sam added, as though not planning on being up to his ankles in soggy water cleanup all day anyway.

"I wanna go through it." Lyla had curiosity written all over her face. So blatant I couldn't help but laugh.

Frankie stood up and stretched. "I'll race you."

"Frankie," I started to tell her it maybe wasn't a good idea, but Lyla cut me off, her dimples—she had dimples—showing.

"On your mark, get set, go!" Byron said, and neither of them hesitated, laughing as they hunched down and scrambled through the ridged metal pipe.

I swung my camera from its case across my back and pulled it out.

When they got to the other side, I called through the echoing tunnel. "Wait there. I'm gonna take a picture."

Lyla was a tiny figure fifty feet away, lit by the sunlight coming through on the other side, framed in the tunnel's circle. Even without a zoom lens, I could tell she was smiling.

With a click, I snapped a picture just as she jerked her head to the right. Then she moved out of my line of sight.

A shriek echoed out of the pipe.

"What is it?" Byron called.

I moved to get a view down the other pipe and could see Frankie and Lyla paused at the opening on the other side.

"Just a squirrel, I think," Lyla called down. "Scared the—"

But something cut her off. ...

"Y'all?" Meara called.

Lyla turned toward us, putting a finger to her lips. All four of us craned our necks to listen. But for what?

Mojito let out a low growl from the back of her throat.

"What is it, Mo?" Sam scratched her behind the ears, but Mojito kept staring down the tunnel.

22

It sounded like water. Rushing water, faint, distant, scratching at the outside of the pipes. Lapping against the metal?

The dog let out another growl then moved so quickly it almost yanked Sam onto his knees.

Was it a familiar sound? Had I heard it before?

It dawned on Frankie first, then a moment later, me.

"Run!" I shouted down the pipe.

Frankie pushed Lyla ahead of her into the pipe just as the quiet rush turned into a shrieking metal crunch. They scrambled halfway down the pipe, when the one Lyla had been in moments before burst and muddy brown water geysered through the side wall, filling the tunnel.

"Faster!" I screamed.

They were almost out. The water in the other tunnel bulged the side of the one they were in, just behind where they were.

Byron and Meara hopped on top of the pipes and reached down, helping Sam up just before the water burst out from the opening where he'd stood seconds before.

Three sets of hands reached for us as the water pushed Lyla and Frankie out from behind. We caught hold and scrambled onto the landing where Byron, Meara, and Sam were.

A pile of soaking teenagers. Breathing fast. Eyes wide.

"Are you okay?" I asked, panting.

Frankie held up her hands, which were scraped bloody. Mojito was jumping on us all and sniffing to make sure we were all right.

"Should have kept my gloves on." Frankie frowned down at her palms.

"Come on. We gotta move," Meara was saying, pulling at us to get up out of the reach of the water, but when we looked down, it was just a steady flow, like we might have seen after a short rainstorm.

"I think it stopped," Byron said, noticing what I had. Whatever had burst, it was somehow over now.

Then Frankie, still out of breath, said grimly, "Guys, where are those skateboarders?"

Chapter 4

The six of us took off running, leaving our bags of trash where they'd fallen, avoiding the drainage ditch we'd walked up so easily earlier, worried more water might rush through.

When we reached the place where the skateboarders had been, they were nowhere to be seen.

"Oh crap, where are they?" Sam asked, looking around the bottom of the culvert.

But there was nothing to see, and already the water was down to just a couple inches high. Mojito knew something was wrong, and her ears were tucked back while she sniffed around.

"Hurry." Frankie rushed onward.

The rest of us worked to keep up, panting as we did.

After a few more yards, she stopped abruptly and turned back toward us just briefly. "Byron, call an ambulance."

She jumped down the edge of the creek, out of sight.

"Oh my god." Meara gasped, rushing after her, the rest of us on her heels.

Byron took out his phone and was dialing when I reached the edge where Frankie had jumped down.

Tangled face down and unmoving at the bottom of the creek, caught in brush, were the two boys we'd seen. The rush of water had pushed them downstream when it gushed out of the pipe.

I leaped down and was at Frankie's side in seconds, both of us reaching to turn the first boy over in the water and get his face out of the muck. First aid classes coursed through my head, and yes, moving someone injured could cause further injury, but being face down in even just an inch of water was a much surer way to die.

As soon as we flipped him face up, I moved onto the next kid, Lyla now by my side, the mud squelching around our knees. The second boy was smaller, and his shoulder was bent at a weird angle. But we moved him face up, and I frantically felt for a pulse.

My fingers were on his throat when he let out a loud cough and spit water all over the front of Lyla's coveralls.

"Are you okay?" I asked, looking around for any blood or gashes, especially on his head in case he had a concussion. I didn't see anything.

He whispered hoarsely, "I think so?"

"Can you sit up?" I asked, and he nodded.

Lyla and I helped him up, and he winced when his shoulder moved. Together, we got him over to the edge, away from the water.

He was still coughing up green water, snot streaming down his nose. He gasped, and gulping in air, asked in a scratchy voice, "Brantley?"

Lyla and I looked over and saw that Frankie and Meara were taking turns performing CPR on the other kid. As soon as our kid saw his friend, he burst into tears.

"What happened to Brantley?" he wailed and tried to stand up to go to him.

"Hey, buddy, it's okay. Sit down. My sister over there is going to help him, okay? And we called an ambulance." I knelt down in front of him and held both his hands. "I want you to just focus on me, okay?"

"Another one bites the dust. *buh buh buh* Another one bites the dust," Frankie sang under her breath as she gave him chest compressions.

"What's she doing? Why is she singing that?" Lyla asked, frowning.

"The beat," I explained quickly. "Our first aid instructor thought it was funny. The beat is the right speed and length for CPR."

"That is so messed up." Lyla shook her head. "But I will never forget it, so I guess it's effective."

"I'm going to help her." I said. "You got him?" I nodded toward the other kid who most certainly had something terribly wrong with his shoulder but was conscious and, while he was still a sobbing mess, he at least didn't seem like he was about to stop breathing.

"Yeah, yeah of course."

Byron called down from the top of the creek bank, "An ambulance is on the way. Sam and I are going to the road so they know how to get here!"

"Hurry," I said.

They both nodded, sprinting away.

Frankie was fully focused on the other kid, and I didn't want to break her concentration. She did maybe three more rounds, but it felt like hours going by in slow motion.

Then, his body gave a violent shake, and his head jerked back. He spewed slick, green mud all over Frankie. She sagged back in relief, wiping the sludge off her mouth and nearly collapsing next to him, and Meara patted the kid on the back, encouraging him to get it all out.

When the paramedics arrived a few minutes later, both boys were in tears but had shakily climbed out of the ditch on their own. The first responders took over, and both of the boys wound up going with them to get checked out.

The teacher sponsor had shown up too and agreed to ride with the boys to the ambulance and talk to their parents.

"It's a good thing you all were here. Did you see what happened?" one paramedic asked as the other two put the boys on stretchers.

"It was like a flash flood or something," I said. Though honestly, I didn't know what had happened. We'd always been warned not to play around in the culverts when it was raining, but in the ten years we'd been exploring them, nothing like this had ever happened.

"Do you know how to get in contact with their parents?" she asked, and we shook our heads.

"We don't know them," Meara said, shivering despite the warmth.

"Well then, it really was lucky you all were here," the paramedic said. "Could we get contact information for one of you? If anything comes up, someone might have some questions."

"Sure, here," I said, writing down my school email on their clipboard.

"Thank you all for your help. You really saved the day." And with that, the ambulance was driving away to meet the boys' parents at the nearest hospital, where they were probably losing their minds with worry.

"I'm gonna go ahead and call this the full four hours of clean up." I looked around, realizing that we'd all left our trash bags behind and were therefore actively undoing any progress that the rest of the students were making.

"We'll go get the bags," Byron said to Sam.

"You sure?" I asked.

"Yeah, it's not that far. We'll catch up." Sam tugged gently at Mo's leash.

I wasn't going to argue. I was bone tired, and I was guessing so was everyone else.

We started walking toward the school parking lot. It was so easy to forget how close we were to just normal school and neighborhood stuff, after all that had just happened.

"You two are basically heroes," I said, giving Frankie and Meara both hugs. "I don't know how you remembered to sing that song."

Frankie shrugged. "The trainer said we should just let the class lesson take over. Become one with our first aid training."

"Well, you saved that kid's life."

"We'll see," Frankie said, a blank look crossing her face. A beat passed, then she was pointing. "What the hell."

The rest of us turned to see what she was pointing at. It was what was left of one of the skateboards, a good hundred yards away from where the boys had been. It was broken in half, like someone really strong had cracked it over their knee, like, a twig.

"How the heck?" Meara muttered.

We had to crane our necks to see it. The board was wedged at least twenty feet up in a tree whose roots spread down the side of the banks and into the water.

I couldn't quite clock what I was seeing, and I didn't think anyone else could either.

Then Lyla pointed to the left. "Look, the other one."

And sure enough. Not five feet away in another tree, but just as high up and equally damaged, was a second skateboard.

"That can't be theirs, right?" Meara shook her head.

"No, no way," I agreed and decided it was time to keep walking. I was worried about Frankie's hands and wanted to make sure she got taken care of quickly.

As we neared the truck, my adrenaline had worn off, and it was like my blood pumping so high had made my body flush out all of my anxiety meds.

I could feel a panic attack coming on, and I tapped Frankie on the elbow to let her know. She nodded and leaned over to whisper something to Meara, who peeled off just as we made it to the truck, and I landed on the ground in front of the bumper.

Frankie pulled off my sweatshirt for me and helped me take my shoes off, my hands shaking so hard I could barely grasp the laces.

"Five things," she said firmly, holding up her hand. "Five things you see."

I couldn't breathe, but I took a breath and closed my eyes for a moment.

"Five things you see, Jean."

I opened my eyes and took another non-breath. "The school."

She nodded encouragingly.

"Your stupid face."

She laughed, and that made me laugh, which helped me breathe.

Meara appeared with a bottle of water and disappeared just as quickly.

After the five-four-three-two-one exercise, my breathing was back to a more normal pace, but my body felt even more drained than it had running from the water and running to the boys.

"I'm not the one who almost died." I felt the shame spiral bearing down on me. Logically, I felt like I shouldn't have any anxiety about this. The boys were the ones who were in danger, not me, but my body was always tricking itself into thinking I was the one in danger.

My therapist said it was like constantly being stuck in a fight-or-flight decision.

"No excuses." Frankie spoke sternly.

I had to say it back, or she wouldn't let me get up. "No excuses."

"Let's go home," Frankie said, pulling me up from the ground.

At some point, most of the other cars had left, and the truck bed was full of the bags and tools.

"That sounds good," I said, handing her my fanny pack so she could get the truck keys out.

Meara, Sam, and Byron were waiting for us so they could help toss the trash bags into the dumpster, and Frankie flashed them a thumbs-up. It occurred to me just then to wonder where Lyla had gone. And what my friends had told her.

But mostly, I was just ready to be in my bed.

Chapter 5

As soon as we got home, I headed straight to the shower with a promise I wouldn't take too much of the hot water, and Frankie gathered up all our clothes to get them put into the washer so all the grime wouldn't set. I thought briefly that I should let Frankie go first, but she insisted.

Our parents were out, so it was just the two of us for a few hours, which I was grateful for because it meant we didn't have to answer a million and one questions about what had happened. Frankie texted them so if they heard anything about the skateboarders and that pipe, they wouldn't worry.

While I was finishing up, I heard a knock on the bathroom door.

"What's up?" I called.

"Mind if I wait in here?" Frankie asked, opening the door a crack.

"Of course not. Come in."

When we were little, we always took our baths and showers together. Then we stopped along the way, but until she got sick, we'd always hang out with each other and talk while the other bathed. We hadn't done that in a while, aside from occasionally popping in to grab a brush or some makeup or to brush our teeth.

I heard her shuffle some things out of the way and hop onto the counter.

"So, that was pretty wild," she said while I rinsed out my shampoo.

"Yeah, I can't believe that pipe burst." I shook a bit as I grabbed the conditioner and put a dollop into my palm.

"I wonder what could have caused it to happen."

"I have no idea. Maybe the city people will have an explanation. We should watch the news, just in case." I had been thinking about what might have happened as I'd been showering. All that water had to have come from somewhere. Then for it to just stop was weird too. I'd read quite a bit about the waterways in our area as part of my environmental club fact finding. It was way easier to get people to fund cleanup projects and things when you could explain what was going on.

"That's a good idea," she said, "to check the news."

"You did amazing out there, Frankie. Giving that kid CPR and finding him and everything." I turned off the water and grabbed the towel to wrap around me as I stepped out.

I glanced over at Frankie, who had a vacant look in her eyes. Clearly as tired as I was from the day. River cleanup always wore me out, but this was next level.

"Want me to hang out while you shower?" I asked.

But she shook her head. "Nah, you go get dressed. Mom said we could order pizza for dinner."

"I'm on it." I nodded. "Movie?"

"Yeah, that sounds good."

Twenty minutes later, we were running the laundry for our clothes, and Inferno's Pizza was on the way. It felt so cozy after the morning and I was worried I'd have trouble staying awake until the pizza came, but I managed.

"To saving the day," I joked, holding my pizza up for a toast.

"To saving the day." Frankie smiled a small smile and took a bite of the mushroom-and-black olive slice. But she made a face when she did, and I paused with my piece halfway to my mouth.

"What's wrong?"

"Blech." She spit the bite out into a napkin.

I examined my slice more closely. One time, another pizza place had put anchovies on our pizza, and I'd thought I was going to never trust melted cheese again. But everything looked normal. And Inferno's had never let us down.

"The mushrooms taste really gross." She set down her slice and started picking them off one by one, putting them into a little white sauce-covered pile.

"You're the one who always insists on mushrooms." I frowned, taking a sniff of mine, but they seemed like regular mushrooms.

"Well, not today." She took a small bite of the now mushroom-free slice.

I looked at mine and decided I would take my chances because all of their pizza was bomb and I would not ruin it.

"What do you want to watch?" I flipped on the TV and took my favorite throw blanket for myself.

"I don't really care." Frankie took the opposite end of the couch and kicked her legs up onto the coffee table.

"How about—"

But she cut me off. "No animal documentaries, Jean."

I pouted for a moment but was too tired to put up much of a fight, even though there was a whole new series about the slow loris and I was adamant about their eyes. They were some fantastic eyes. But I compromised, and we went with a comfort film.

We started the movie, and after the first five minutes of *What We Do in the Shadows* and three slices of pizza, I must have fallen asleep because I woke up with the credits rolling and Luce curled up on half of my face. She gave me a withering side-eye when I lifted my head off the pillow.

Frankie sat upright, staring at the screen in the same unseeing way that she had been before in the bathroom.

"Frankie?" I mumbled, wiping the drool from the side of my face and thinking I probably should have seen a doze coming and brought in my bed pillow. "Frankie?"

I had to call her name two more times before she blinked and shook her head, looking away from the TV.

"You awake?" I asked, sitting up and reaching for the pizza box. She'd barely touched her slice.

Finally, she nodded and said, "Yeah, just tired, I think."

"Me too. Let's go to bed." I took her hand, giving her a pull up. On the way to our room, I stuck the pizza box in the fridge, noticing that it was barely eight o'clock but fully expecting I'd be able to sleep hard.

I practically fell into my bottom bunk and heard Frankie climb up the wooden rungs and do the same onto her top bunk.

"Night, Frankie," I muttered, my eyelids already heavy with sleep.

"Night, Jean," she mumbled back then clicked her lamp off.

The next morning, we had a lot of questions to answer from our parents, who I had heard come in to check on us when they got home from a dinner with some friends just after ten.

Usually, they would just peek their heads in, but they actually took the time to walk in and give us both sleepy kisses on the forehead, so I knew they must have heard about what had happened. I was grateful they waited until morning to ask us about it. And they had made breakfast, so I was shoveling some turkey bacon and pancakes along with my coffee, while Frankie and I filled them in.

After we finished, they told us how proud they were of us and how lucky those boys were that we were there.

"I just hope I don't have to do that ever again." Frankie shuddered involuntarily.

"I hope not too, sweetheart." Ma rested a hand on Frankie's head.

I was grateful that Frankie had left out the part about me having a full-blown panic attack at the end. Our folks worried about my anxiety so much, and it had been so long since I'd had a bad episode. I didn't even have to ask her to keep it between us. She just did.

"Are you both staying put today," Ma asked, "or do you have plans?"

I answered, "Staying put."

Just as Frankie said, "We have plans."

I shot her a quick look, one of the ones that made our parents swear up and down was a twin look and that they were pretty sure we had some sort of telepathy between us.

Like we were twins but I just took an extra eighteen months to gestate like a manatee.

"Oh yeah, plans," I said, not really worried about being super convincing and also hoping whatever Frankie needed wouldn't take long. I was still tired from my panic attack and the general drama of yesterday. Though I owed her for conveniently leaving out the panic attack part, I was woefully behind on homework and had planned on wrangling at least a few of my friends to study with me.

"Okay, well, stay safe, whatever you do, and be back for dinner." Mom gave me a quick hug. "And Frankie, take it easy."

Frankie gave them a thumbs-up and headed to our room. I refilled my rainbow cat coffee mug and followed her, accepting hugs from both our moms on my way out of the kitchen, Lucifer weaving between our legs as we climbed the stairs. I swore that cat was going to trip me some day and be all "I mean, you should have paid more attention" about it.

When I got to our room, Frankie was pulling on a pair of work pants and her rain boots.

"So, where are we going?" I asked. "And more importantly, do I have time to drink my coffee, or should I get a thermos?"

"Yes to the second one, and we're going to look at that pipe."

That gave me pause. "Um, pretty sure they roped that whole thing off? Which is what our folks said? The road and everything?"

"Well, yeah but that's for cars. We can get closer than that on foot."

I frowned. "There's no way it's safe."

She crossed her arms. "It wasn't ever safe, apparently, but we played down there eight trillion times with nothing bad happening. What are the chances something bad happens two days in a row?"

"Right, well, that sounds like famous last words territory you're skipping into, Frankie."

I could tell she had made up her mind, and it was going to be one of those classic, "Fine, I'll go by myself then" moments if I said no.

Plus, being honest, I was really curious. Not quite so eager—I would have been fine waiting a month to look at it, or at least until Monday after school—but I definitely wanted to see what it looked like now that the water had drained and if there was going to be any bad effects on the park and creek downstream because of it.

"Okay, let me finish this coffee though," I said, "and I can't forget to take my meds."

As if she'd been waiting, she tossed me my med bag and water bottle. "I got you, sis."

Frankie grinned, and I groaned. She could get me to do anything.

"You know I hate when you play the big sister card so effortlessly," I said.

"Want me to lay your clothes out?"

"Fine, sure." I gave in, laughing, getting dressed and grabbing my camera bag. I unzipped the case to check the amount of frames I had left. Five to go, which was perfect. I would use them today and get the film development started during my afternoon block on Monday. Film was pricey. I didn't want to just blow through rolls, but I was so excited to work the darkroom it was hard not to.

We hollered goodbyes to our folks and pulled the door shut behind us, heading back to the culvert.

When we got there, we saw quickly that we weren't the only ones with the same idea.

Chapter 6

"Guessing you all had the same idea as us?" Frankie stepped up next to Meara and Byron, who were both standing hesitantly at the opening of the pipe. Meara looped her arm through Frankie's elbow.

The road above the pipe was completely blocked off by cones where it ran under the road, but it wasn't exactly tricky to get to the opening just like we had the day before. It was going to make traffic before school on Monday a total nightmare though, and I was grateful we lived close enough to walk.

"Have y'all gone in to look at it yet?" My brain was bouncing between whether I should go focus on homework, my actual plan for the day, and giving totally into curiosity about what in the world had happened and if we were in immediate danger.

But now that Meara and Byron were here, I would have been down a couple potential study buddies anyway, so I'd just do my best to rope them into it later on in the day.

Byron shook his head. "Not sure I'm going to."

"Same," I agreed.

Frankie crouched down and cocked her head, listening.

"Do you hear anything?" Meara asked softly.

Frankie shook her head. "Nothing. Let's go look."

"Are we actually sure that's a good idea? Seems like it's tempting fate. What if it's, like, a sinkhole or something like they said on the news and we all go falling into it?" Byron crossed his arms with a scowl.

Frankie picked up a stick from the side of the drain and gave the pipe a loud thwack. "Seems solid to me."

"Oh, sure, real scientific, Frankie." I crossed my arms too.

"Should we have brought a rope?" Frankie shrugged and took a few steps into the tunnel.

The drain had no more water than the day before, and we could see sunlight streaming in from the other side. But there was clearly something different thanks to the giant gap in the middle. There didn't seem to be anything wrong with the road, but I assumed cave-ins were a potential threat.

"All right, I'm going in. You coming?" Meara asked and, crouching down, scurried ahead of Frankie in the tunnel where the water had burst.

"Wait for me," Frankie said, following her.

"Slow down, you two." Byron ducked in after them.

I didn't want Frankie to go without me, so taking a deep breath and reminding myself of the literally dozens of times we'd crawled through without any issues, I crawled in as well, grouchy I was going to most certainly be forced to do more laundry today.

I'm glad I went, though, because having to get one of them to explain what we were seeing would have been really difficult.

When we got to almost the center of the pipe, the damage was blatant.

Stacked up like cartoon characters, we all got a closer look at it, Meara and Frankie making room for me and Byron to see.

"Creepy," Meara said.

Frankie pulled a flashlight out of her inner jean jacket pocket and clicked it on.

The place where the water had burst was now an open hole. The metal of the pipes bent out, curling like flower petals away from the opening. A small portion of the pipe at the bottom was missing, but for the most part, other than the ten-foot-long gash in the side, it seemed intact.

Frankie scooched over so she and Meara could see into the hole better.

"What's in there?" Byron asked.

But they both shrugged.

Frankie swung the flashlight back and forth. "It just looks mostly like dirt and roots, but it goes a ways back."

"I can't tell where the water came from." I moved forward to see better, but it really did just look like a short tunnel. Sort of like the half caves that were created in the swampy part of the park where the water eroded the dirt near the side, but the tree roots kept the top part in place.

There was more cement and pipes, but none of it was as cleared out as the one we were crouched in.

"Me neither," Byron agreed. "Can I see your flashlight?"

"Sure," Frankie handed it to him.

I took out my camera. Setting the exposure as high as I could, I rested the camera on the ground to steady it and snapped a picture, aiming into the dark shadow of the cave.

Frankie and Byron moved the flashlight around, but nothing screamed out of the ordinary.

"Say cheese." I took a picture of Meara and Frankie crouched by the opening.

"How did it tear like this?" Meara ran a finger along the edge of one of the ribboned metal tears. She tapped her knuckle against it, and though it looked like it was thin, the metal didn't move at all. As though it was always in that position or someone had sculpted it that way.

"That's a good question." Frankie pursed her lips.

"This is weird, right?" I asked. The hairs on the back of my neck were basically in a perpetual state of rise, and I had a flash of remembering the sound of the water coming down the pipes, which made me shiver.

"Yeah, yeah, this is weird," Byron agreed.

"I'm out," I decided. "It's giving me the creeps."

Byron and I crawled out of the tunnel. I stood at the exit, stretching my legs. We both crouched down when a car drove up and had to turn around because of the roadblock. I really didn't want to get in trouble for playing around here. The most they could probably do was yell at us, but I didn't want to have any sort of adult confrontation on a weekend morning.

"Y'all coming?" Byron called down the passage.

I took a picture of him, framed in the opening.

"Hey, at least get my good side." He laughed and struck a pose, which I also captured.

"All your sides are good sides, Byron."

"Come on. We're hungry," he called again.

"We are?" I asked.

"I just assumed."

"I mean, you're not wrong."

Meara and Frankie made their way out a few minutes later, and the four of us walked together, taking the long way back to Byron's house through the park.

Part way home, Frankie stopped. "I want to get them."

"Huh?" I asked, my tummy giving a rumble loud enough that Byron heard and laughed.

"Told you," he said.

I ignored him. "What do you want to get?"

Then I looked up to where Frankie was pointing. We'd stopped at the tree where the first of the two skateboards was stuck in the branches.

"Why? They're shredded." Byron frowned, covering his eyes and squinting up.

"Souvenirs?" Frankie shrugged. "For the memories?"

"Fine, but then we eat." I helped her scramble up the side of the creek, pulling ourselves up by the roots exposed against the wall of dirt. They were even more prominent than the day before because of the huge rush of water that pushed through this way.

When we got to the top, maybe ten feet up from the creek bed, I gave her a bit of a boost, and she was able to grab the lowest branches, pulling herself up the rest of the way and climbing until she could reach the branch where the skateboard, or what was left of it, was wedged. With a big shake of the end, the board came loose, and despite my repeated warnings about concussions and that the boards were already destroyed, Meara and Byron stood below, ready to catch it.

Which Meara did, gratefully not knocking either of them out.

"Y'all, this is weird too," Byron called as Frankie and I climbed back down the side.

Weird was an understatement. The skateboard looked like it had been through a blender, but it was still all connected to itself. The wood was like ribbons, bent and twisted in impossible

43

knots. The metal of the trucks and the wheels spun around like a wrung-out washcloth.

"Think the other one is like this?" I looked over at the second board that was harder to reach than the first and hoped Frankie's curiosity was satisfied with just the one.

"What, just held together by the deck grip?" Byron took the skateboard from Meara and examined it.

"You gonna keep it?" Meara asked Frankie.

"It's kinda cool," Frankie said.

"Not sure 'cool' is the word I would use but sure," I said. "Hold it up. It can be your trophy for saving those kids."

Frankie laughed, and I made the three of them line up, holding the skateboard tumbleweed like they had just won a tournament.

As I wound the shutter, I felt the familiar pull of a roll of film being finished, and I quickly wound it up to make sure I didn't accidentally ruin my first roll of the year.

"Okay, now can we eat something?" I asked.

We walked the rest of the way to Byron's, where his mom provided endless cases of cup-o-ramen. He and I had spicy chicken flavor cups while Meara and Frankie examined the skateboard.

"I wonder if we could unravel it?" Meara mused.

"I mean, we could try," Frankie agreed, the two of them more focused than I'd just about ever seen them.

"Hey, have you heard from those kids' parents?" Byron asked.

I shook my head. "I hope they're both doing okay."

"I'm sure they're fine." Meara looked at the ball of skateboard, holding her chin in one hand like it was a logic puzzle.

"Right, well, good luck with your unraveling," I said. "I have, like, seventy hours of homework to finish, so I'm going to head home."

"Want me to walk you?" Frankie asked, but I shook my head. "No, it's still just three minutes away. I'll be fine."

I had walked the four doors down a trillion times. I wondered why Frankie had decided to be extra protective until I remembered my panic attack yesterday.

So I gave her an extra thumbs-up. "For real, I'll see you when you get home."

She nodded, and Byron walked me to the door.

"Are they acting kinda strange to you?" Byron asked softly as we got to the front porch.

Glancing back at the two of them studying the ball of wood, I shrugged. "Not more than usual."

His frown was pensive.

"Hey." I put my hand on his arm and gave it a squeeze. "Yesterday was absolutely bonkers. We're all kinda shook up."

"Yeah, yeah, that's probably it." He put his hand on top of mine and gave it a quick squeeze. "Anyway, you want to study together later?"

I nodded vigorously. "Please, yes."

"I'll come over around two then." Byron gave me a thumbs-up.

"I'll see you later." I pulled the door behind me and headed home to deal with the nightmarish amount of calculus homework I had looming over the rest of my weekend.

The socks you're wearing squish when you take a step. Water pools at your feet, soaking into your pants.

Realizing that it's your pants that are making the puddle, you take a step back. Your socks squish again but this time in mud.

There is little light where you stand.

An animal whines to your left. You cock your head to listen.

It is not in pain.

You take a step forward, back toward the spot where the puddle is. There is less mud there.

The smell of water is close by. You've been here before.

Peeling off your socks with one hand, you set them down in the puddle.

Your feet are now bare. You walk toward the task at hand.

Chapter 7

Our Monday morning routine started without a hitch. Then Frankie and I got to the entrance to the school, and suddenly we, along with our friends, were the center of attention from everyone who hadn't been at the cleanup day. Between the news coverage, the street closure, and it being in the general ether of social media, our entire school knew part of what had gone on and wanted to personally question us about any details they might have missed hearing about.

"For real." Meara looked at Frankie and me, eyebrows raised. "Should we go hide out in the bathroom until class starts?"

I looked at Frankie. We were clearly both considering it. In a school that was big enough to let you both excel and simultaneously fade into the background, we were not at all used to being the center of gossip or peppered with inquiries. I especially worried about Frankie since there had been so much unwanted attention when she'd gotten back to school after being sick. It took people awhile to stop asking her tons of questions.

I got to my first class even earlier than usual because I was tired of answering questions about the catastrophic—okay, that might be a bit of an exaggeration—creek clean up on Saturday.

Word had spread quickly about the event, though somehow Blakely and Jack had a much larger part in what had happened by the time the rumors got going. That was fine with me. Let them have any attention that would otherwise be pointed toward myself. I was already anxious about how many people had asked me what had happened, and the day had barely begun.

Blakely had a good idea to push sign-ups for the next event though, and she was right. The Environmental Protection Club had never been high on the popular clubs list at our school. Granted, it was fueled by the innate desire to be part of something interesting, and I felt like people should be interested in the environment all the time, not just when random pipes went all Yosemite out of nowhere.

I got permission from my homeroom teacher to print off a few sign-ups and spent the last half of my first period tacking them up on the various bulletin boards around the school, hitting up the library, cafeteria, and offices.

When I got to the front office, a familiar face greeted me.

"Lyla," I whispered toward her as I tacked the printout to the bulletin board. Sure, the front office was technically not like a quiet space and I'd been on a first name basis with every attendance secretary we'd had at the school since I started here, but I was erring on the side of hushed chatter. "You're not in trouble, are you?"

She laughed, and the gentle sound it made was exceedingly pleasant. "No," Lyla replied in an exaggerated stage whisper. "I'm just getting my schedule finalized because some of my info didn't get here before I started. Transfer, remember?"

"Oh yeah, that makes sense. Are you happy with most of your classes so far?" I went back to speaking at a normal volume, though I wondered what whispering into her ear would be like. I knew full well that she had exactly zero classes with me, and my stomach did a flippy flop at the possibility there might be a schedule shuffle that had some of our classes overlap.

She nodded and handed me a copy. After whatever changes she and her counselor had come up with, one hour overlapped with mine.

"Hope it's okay, I kinda decided to take yearbook?" Suddenly, she looked shy.

I would've sworn the goofy grin on my face was one look from her away from cracking my cheeks open. "Of course! That's awesome."

She smiled and took the paper back. "What are you doing up here?"

I pointed to the sign-up sheet. "Blakely thinks like a politician. She figured we should use the momentum about what happened on Saturday to get more people signed up for the next clean up."

Lyla shrugged. "I mean, that makes sense. Nothing folks respond to more than FOMO."

"True." Then a thought occurred to me—and by "thought," I mean some sort of out-of-control social dynamo replacing my mouth—and I asked, "Want to come to the darkroom with me?"

Immediately followed by another thought occurring to me that what I'd just said sounded super weird and possibly creepy. Because darkrooms were dark and niche, and I was maybe cool in a weird way, but that did not always translate to weird in a good way.

As if seeing that thought displayed across my face like a banner trailing off a tiny airplane, Lyla gave me a thumbs-up. "After last period?"

I nodded.

"I'd love to. I've never used one before."

"Me neither." I backed out of the office in a super cool way that included bumping into the door frame a bit but not quite enough to turn into a full-on tripping incident. "See you in class, then. Gotta get back before the bell rings."

She gave me another thumbs-up, which I was starting to recognize as being her response to me being a total dork.

And then, to make my exceedingly not cool exit better, my counselor poked her head out of her office and said, "Hey Jean, I was about to make an appointment with you. Could you step into my office for a sec?"

So, I got to walk back past Lyla.

After saying goodbye already.

Because leaving one room to get into another was such a freaking struggle.

"Hey, Mrs. K. What's up?" I asked when I got in the counselor's office.

"Take a seat." She gestured at the door, and I pulled it closed behind me. "I just want to talk to you about Frankie for a second."

"Okay." I sat down and set the clipboard I was holding in my lap so I could fidget with a pen while we talked. I was immediately on edge, running a thousand worried scenarios through my head. "What's up?"

Mrs. K let out a big sigh. "I'm just worried that Frankie is going to self-sabotage her chances of getting into the college she wants to. She does so well on her exams and yet keeps refusing to apply herself as fully as I think she could."

"Frankie isn't going to college," I told her. Surely, she'd gotten more than one earful from Frankie over the last three years about her thoughts on academia.

"I don't know if that's the right choice for her. She would do so well in an academic setting post high school." Mrs. K continued. "Don't you imagine the two of you going to college together?"

"I mean, it's crossed my mind." I frowned. This conversation seemed like one she should be having with Frankie.

"Just know that, if there is anything you can do to help me nudge Frankie in that direction, I would be so grateful. She has so much potential." Mrs. K seemed like she wanted me to elaborate or agree with her, but I just wanted to wrap up the conversation.

"I'll see what I can do." But I wasn't sure what I *could* do. Or if I wanted to do anything. I wanted what was best for Frankie. I always did. Maybe Mrs. K was right, and I was the person who could get through to her.

I made it back to class right before the end of first period with a pass from Mrs. K and a lot to think about. The rest of the first half of the day dragged. It didn't help speed things up that I was literally sweating with excitement about developing film in the darkroom.

Why did so many things make me sweaty? Ugh.

When it got to be lunchtime, I got a text from Blakely, excited to announce we'd already had, like, seventeen new people sign up for the next cleanup.

I suggested we may need more adults there, but Blakely just sent back a sunshine and a lemon emoji, which I did not have any idea how to interpret.

Finding Meara and Sam in the usual spot, I took my seat next to them and looked around to see if Lyla had the same lunch period as us. But if she did, she wasn't in the cafeteria. Which was valid. The food was rather dubious at times. Except on chicken fried steak days. Those days were sacred.

"Hey, Sam, I feel like I haven't seen you in forever." I started pulling out my lunch box and munching on some carrots.

"Yeah, Meara said y'all went to the pipes yesterday. What was that like?" he asked, offering us both some beef jerky. I took a piece and popped it in my mouth.

"It was so weird. The metal is just, like, shredded." I fanned out my fingers to show the shape as best I could. "I took some pictures I can show you later if the developing works."

"Cool. I want to go check it out too."

"Just don't get in trouble. We're not supposed to be around there in case it turns out to be a sinkhole. Can't have us getting buried alive or anything."

He nodded. "My folks are so annoyed that the road is still closed. I bet they all complain enough that the city moves the cones in, like, a day."

"Or until someone moves the stuff out of the way themselves. Or, like, drives over it with a truck."

"I saw an article about a sink hole in Florida that ate up an entire block. Just like, poof, street gone," Sam made magic-trick hands at me.

My moms had told us the neighborhood social media page was being flooded with complaints about it. Though it was kinda hard to tell how many people were actually upset, since the loudest folks took up the most space on there.

"Meara, you okay?" I nudged her lunch with a carrot. "You're being really quiet."

She gave a small shrug. "Just not hungry."

"Got anything good in there?" I asked.

She pushed the lunch box over to me. "Go nuts. Just leave the sandwich in case I get hungry later."

"Yo! You sure?" Sam said and grinned at the contents. Takis and baklava. Meara's folks always had the best snacks and desserts out of all of our grownups. He and I split them both, and before we knew it, lunch was over.

Chapter 8

It was finally time for last period, and I tried not to trip in my hurry to the yearbook room.

For once, the butterflies in my stomach didn't seem to be totally anxiety related, which was both confusing and exciting. My therapist had me doing some exercises to differentiate between anxiety and anticipation. Being anxious was like always being in anticipation of the worst thing. Just being excited about something had a lot of the same symptoms, at least in my body.

So yeah, deep breaths.

Meds were working.

I'd eaten a good lunch.

With plenty of protein.

These were happy feelings.

Still.

Even sorting it out was getting me anxious, so I was glad that when I got to the yearbook room, Lyla was already at a station, which happened to be next to the one I always used so I didn't have to do the awkward where are you gonna sit conversation in my brain.

Her back was to me, and she was focusing hard on the computer in front of her. I could tell from across the room that she was finishing up the spread on the volleyball teams. Mrs. Camp must have gotten her started right away, or else she had yearbook experience already.

I walked up behind her, and when she still didn't turn around, I tapped her on the shoulder and said, "Hey."

She screamed. Like, full-blown shrieked and jumped up, knocking the chair onto its side and bumping into the desk so hard the computer shook.

"Whoa, hey, hey, it's me." I stepped back and held up my hands.

"Holy crap, Jean, you scared the bugs outta me." Lyla was laughing nervously now and trying to catch her breath.

I stepped up to her. "I am so sorry I scared you."

"No, it's fine. I've just been…" She glanced around the room as if she was figuring out where she was. "Jumpy, I guess?"

"Seems like it." I reached down to set the chair back up.

Only about four other kids were in the class already, and two of them had their headphones in and didn't even glance up. I swore the room could be on fire and half the teenagers in this school would be so busy doing their best to zone out they wouldn't even notice.

Side benefit of generalized anxiety was I never got that luxury, so I'd be able to rescue everyone in a timely manner.

Lyla took a few seconds to steady her breathing and heart rate. I knew if mine was up, hers had to be.

"I'm surprised none of the teachers came when you yelled." I glanced out the open classroom door.

"I'd rather not have an audience." She laughed.

"Those are looking good, by the way." I smiled, pointing to her work. "Did you do yearbook at your old school?"

Lyla nodded. "I was a junior editor at my yearbook last year. I loved it. I'm really glad your teacher let me in."

"Mrs. Camp is the best." Which was my truth. She was one of the coolest teachers I'd ever had, and this year's yearbook was going to be so rad. I knew it.

"I kinda sensed that." Lyla turned back toward her computer. "Better get what summer sports pages done that I can."

"The most important of the things." I took my desk next to hers, and we both got to work. Before we knew it, the bell was ringing, and by the time I finished up the captions I was polishing, the rest of the students had cleared out.

"They really do like to get out of here." Lyla stretched and looked around the empty class.

"Truly," I agreed.

Mrs. Camp came to let us know she had bus duty but would be back later if we needed anything.

"Ready to develop some photos?" I stretched and stood up from where I had hunched at the computer all of class.

We made our way to the back of the classroom, where the darkroom was located. Primarily used for storage now, since all the yearbook photography was digital, it still had all the major equipment. I'd saved up and bought some of the supplies I needed, like, processing liquid and photo paper, and most of what we needed was in good shape.

"You sure you're not too jumpy to be in a dark closet with me?" I asked. "I did scare the crap out of you just an hour ago."

"Is there a lock?"

"Yeah, there is." I frowned. I had been joking, but Lyla was clearly still very jumpy. "There's also a light we can flip on that says not to come in, if you don't want to lock the door."

I couldn't tell if she wanted there to be a lock or not. It was all making my hands kinda sweaty.

She nodded but then seemed relieved when we got to the closet and there was in fact a latch on the inside. Presumably because high school kids aren't exactly known to be the most observant and I was guessing it was put in after one too many ruined rolls of film.

"You don't mind, do you?" She pulled the door closed and slid in the lock.

I shook my head. "No, that's fine. If you're not comfortable with this, you can go."

"What, and miss out on the most important roll of film of Jean's entire life?" she said it with such a straight face that mine broke into a smile. "When you're a famous photographer, I'm going to brag about this first roll at every single cocktail party I attend for the rest of my life."

"In that case, I guess the lock is a good idea." I laughed and began putting out the supplies we needed to start the development process. "Wouldn't want to brick my most collectible roll. Also, make sure your phone is off. We don't want someone calling and the light turning on."

We spent the next few hours processing the film. I talked Lyla through the process so it took a bit longer than it might have if I'd been working solo, but I was pretty sure I'd done everything correctly since I was going slowly. By the time the film roll was developed and we'd gotten half a dozen prints made, the glowing red lights on the clock wall made it feel like I'd blinked and all of a sudden we were forward in time.

"Oops. I didn't realize how late it is." I gave the counters one last wipe down and warned Lyla that I was going to flip on the lights. It was jarring to suddenly be flooded with the florescent overhead ones after the dim red we were used to.

"Oh, wow, that went fast." Lyla picked up her backpack and handed me mine. "Are you late for something?"

"Just dinner with my folks, and I told Frankie to wait for me after detention."

"Frankie got detention?" Lyla asked with a bit of a laugh.

"Typical, right?" I was suddenly slightly defensive.

"Whoa, no, I'm just surprised. She seems smart enough to stay out of trouble." Lyla shrugged. I liked how she picked up on my prickliness.

"Actually, she did it on purpose." I laughed and liked that she walked with me to the other side of the school to meet up with Frankie. "Our English class read *The Great Gatsby* over the summer, and she decided to have a sit in the first week of school to protest."

"She wanted to protest *The Great Gatsby*?" Lyla laughed. We weren't in the same English class, but everyone had to read it eventually.

"Yeah, she kept chanting the names of Black authors and women and queer writers and artists who have lesser-known books during the same time period as F. Scott."

"That's wild." Lyla gaped at me.

"That's Frankie."

"So, what pushed it to detention?" Lyla asked.

"Oh, she handcuffed herself to a desk, saying she wasn't going anywhere until the curriculum was changed."

"Holy crap." Lyla laughed. "Your sister is a badass."

I rolled my eyes but was maybe more than a little proud. "Don't tell her that. It'll get to her head."

I looked at the prints we'd hung up on a clothesline to dry.

The first was of Meara fluffing out Sam's hair after the first day of school. I loved how it had turned out. They seemed so relaxed in the photo, Meara leaning against the wall of the pavilion roof, Sam in a half grin, his eyes closed.

Two more were of Frankie and Byron, one from behind walking side by side across the field toward Stonefish Creek Park. The other, I'd scurried in front of them to take from the other side. Frankie had her tongue out and had closed her eyes on purpose. Byron was turned toward her, mouth open and laughing.

I must have done something wrong with the last two, however. They were the day after the pipe explosion, and I'd taken a few looking down the tunnel. The negatives looked fine, but something had gone off in the development.

The left edge of both looked like when an old film burned up in a projector. Sort of eroded away.

"Not sure what happened here." I cocked my head and studied both images. "Probably something with the enlarger?"

"Come on, Jean. Three fabulous shots and prints on your first try. Amazing." Lyla elbowed me a bit, and I smiled.

"Okay, that's true, but you have to help me figure out what happened here." I gestured toward the other two.

"Of course." She smiled at me. "Any time."

We walked out together and met up with Frankie as she and the other kids were leaving detention.

"Living that *Breakfast Club* dream, Frankie?" I asked and looped my arm through hers.

"You know it." She saw who I was walking with. "Well, hello there, Lyla, and what brings you here today?"

The blush to my cheeks was immediate, and I know Frankie saw it.

But thankfully, Lyla just said, "We developed some film. Your sister is a really great photographer."

And that got Frankie's attention. "Let me see!"

"You're gonna have to wait until tomorrow. They're drying." I wished that weren't the case but alas.

"Boo, Frankie wants photos now." She swung me around and dragged me back toward the yearbook room.

"Frankie, no, we're gonna be so late for dinner." But I was following her.

"I'll see you tomorrow, Jean," Lyla called from where we'd sort of left her in the hallway.

"See ya tomorrow!" I called back as Frankie pulled me to the darkroom.

When we got there, she stopped abruptly at the threshold, looking in. Then she walked slowly to the hanging images.

"Well," I asked softly, "what do you think?"

"You have a very good eye, Jean." She reached up and ran a finger gently down the part of the image in the pipe that divided the correctly developed portion to the part that messed up.

"I'm still working out the kinks." I bit my lip, nervous for Frankie's approval.

"You're already great at it." Frankie turned and stepped toward me, giving me a fierce hug out of nowhere. I hugged her back. "Let's get home before the folks come after us."

Chapter 9

Two days passed where I wasn't able to find time to work on developing and printing my photos. Mrs. Camp wasn't sure what could have caused the burning effect on my prints and suggested I do another roll of film before we tried anything else to fix it.

So, I was taking my time, looking for shots to take, walking home, when I heard something out of place. I hurried down the path to the sound of barking. When I rounded the corner, Sam and Byron were pulling on Mojito's leash, trying to keep her away from something.

"What is going on?" I yelled, and the two of them turned briefly.

"Mojito won't listen," Sam shouted. Byron was helping him hold the dog back, but they were clearly struggling.

"Here, let me help." I put down my backpack and grabbed the leash so Sam could get to Mo's harness. Mo was a big dog and one of the most well-behaved ones I'd ever met in my entire life. I'd never seen her not listen to a command on the first try.

"What's wrong, doggo?" Sam asked, finally resorting to just picking Mojito up. I didn't know how he could lift the sixty-pound pet while she was straining to get at something.

As soon as she was in Sam's arms, her barks turned to whining and a loud whimper, though her tail was wagging like she was super excited about something.

"What is it, girl?" Byron asked, scratching her behind her good-doggo fluffy ears. She gave him a giant lick right on the chin in response.

Byron and I peered around, trying to see what in the world was making the dog totally lose her noodles.

"I'm gonna take her home," Sam said, and at the sound of the word home, Mojito's whines turned louder, and her tail began to wag vigorously.

"Guess she likes that idea? Maybe?" I kept peering out into the trees.

"I'll see you both later. I gotta go before my arms give out." Sam took off, lugging Mojito with him like she was a giant, fluffy baby. "Thanks for helping me."

"Of course, no problem," Byron said. He and Sam had both broken a sweat.

"How long was she freaking out?" I asked, once Sam was out of earshot.

"Like ten full minutes. It was so weird. We got out of last period early and went to get her for a walk, and everything was normal until we got here."

"Do you know what she was so intent on getting to?" I asked, but Byron shook his head.

"Let's go see if we can find whatever it was." Byron veered off the path and stepped onto the soft undergrowth, heading in the direction Mo had focused in on.

Leaving my backpack on a fallen log, not wanting to sweat even more than I already knew I would, I followed. "Maybe it was, like, a raccoon or a squirrel?"

"Yeah, probably. But she wasn't acting like she does when she's excited. It was more like she wanted me and Sam to go with her."

After about a hundred yards, we still had seen nothing that could have made her act like she had been. I kept expecting a small herd of deer or a mountain lion or something to pop out. Last year, a cougar had escaped from an animal rescue safari place and almost ate a whole dog off its owner's leash. A much smaller dog than Mojito but still. That weenie dog was very freaked out when the cougar got scared off and dropped him, miraculously unharmed.

"Let's turn back," I tapped Byron on the arm, and he turned.

Then became very still.

"What is it?" I turned to follow his gaze.

Through the trees, looking back toward the way we'd come, I squinted. The sun was setting, and the branches cast many shadows.

But there was no wind. And beyond the path, one shadow moved.

I sucked in a breath.

"Did you see that?" Byron asked, barely above a whisper.

I nodded, though I wasn't sure what I was seeing.

At the base of the trees across the water, it looked wrong somehow. I didn't think I'd ever held so still in my life.

We stood there for what felt like a million breaths. The air that had been so cool and gentle was suddenly stifling, as though the lack of wind was mocking us. The humidity settled thick in the cold sweat on the back of my neck.

We waited to see what was going to emerge from behind a tree or fallen log.

But nothing moved again.

Suddenly, the sound of the park came rushing back. I hadn't realized that the birds and bugs and even water had seemed to completely become muted. The smallest breeze kicked up, and several birds flew from a nearby tree. An airplane passed overhead.

"Let's go." Byron said and slowly walked back to the path.

"What was that?" I whispered as we went back the way we'd come.

"I don't know, but you saw it, right?" he asked again.

"Yeah, like a shadow moved." I would have been happy to skip the exploration part of whatever we were doing right then, but I needed my backpack and I'd left it on the path.

I barely kept my eyes on where I was going, focusing straight ahead. There was a large black spot that I thought was a shadow, but as we got closer, whatever it was remained darker than the rest of the shadows.

"We gotta check it out, right?" Byron said softly as we got to the path.

The shadow that had maybe moved was across a swampier part of the creek pond area. I wouldn't have believed I'd seen what it seemed like I had seen, if Byron hadn't also been there. So, we had a couple of options. One was going all the way around and approaching the blob from the other side, or we could make our way across. We'd done it many times, but it always wound up ruining whatever shoes we had on, and I wasn't totally convinced we should even get close to whatever it was.

But Byron was already taking off his shoes and socks and setting them by my backpack.

"Seriously?" I pulled mine off too and set them next to his, rolling up my pants.

This part of the water was like a marsh. There were taller places of dirt and mossy grass that were created when the water wound around the easiest path and was shallow enough not to cover them all. Depending on the year and how much rain we were getting, the paths across would change. It was clear that much of it had eroded after the pipe burst.

In bolder, younger days, we'd challenge each other to races across that usually ended with one or more of us soaked. In hindsight, after learning that so much of the water came from runoff in the neighborhoods and roads, I was surprised none of us had gotten ill from accidentally swallowing some of it over the summers. Not to mention the periods of time where a portion of it became stagnant. We really shouldn't have been playing in that water, but either our parents didn't realize what we were doing or they made a choice to let us have our adventures.

"Ladies first." Byron gestured toward the other side.

"Oh, yeah, sure, no problem," I took a small jump across the gap and made it to a larger, raised area without any issues. Followed closely by Byron, I led us across, calculating each next step as I got there.

The marshy part was about a hundred yards wide, and we made it over quicker than I really wanted to, given how uneager I was to see what we'd seen up close. But as we made our way across, the darker shadow wasn't moving, so I was quickly rationalizing it into general jumpiness.

We were about five feet away from it when the smell hit us.

"Oh jeez." Byron turned his head and wretched.

"Eww." I coughed and gagged, trying to keep myself from throwing up the banana I'd eaten on my walk to the creek.

I pulled up my shirt, covering my nose and mouth with the fabric. It did not totally block the smell, but it helped. My eyes were watering, and I had to force myself to look over at the thing.

"It's gotta be something dead, right?" Byron was doing the same as me.

"Yeah, gotta be." The smell was of stagnant rot and decay. Sickly sweet like the time there was a dead mouse under the refrigerator and we hadn't been able to find it for ages because it had crawled into a metal plate attached to the backside of the fridge.

I looked around until I found what I was searching for and, shaking a few leaves off it, used a long stick to reach over the small gap between us and the large clearly-not-a-shadow but definitely-something-weird thing and gave it a poke.

What had started out looking like a giant, black throw blanket immediately began to dissolve and run into the water below it as soon as I poked it with the stick. It was squelchy like mud and flowed down in chunks like an entire batch of Jell-O going down a disposal.

I backed up as far as I could, still watching whatever it was run into the water. As it did, the ground on which we stood swayed, like we were standing on a raft in a shallow pool. A ripple went across the marsh, and I grabbed Byron to stay standing. But it was over as soon as the whatever-it-was went into the water.

The smell went with it too, and we were able to breathe again without covering our faces.

"What in the world is that?" Byron asked what I was thinking, looking into the water where the muddy blackness had almost disappeared.

I poked the stick into the water where it had slid in, and when I pulled it up, there were long, stringy, black hairs attached to the end of it. The same hairs were along the bank of the water. Like the branches in the side of the creek were a comb, collecting dead hairs as the shadow slipped into the water.

"I have no idea."

Chapter 10

After getting home and showering, I went to bed pretty early and was sleeping hard until Frankie patted me on the shoulder and said, "Hey, Jean, wake up."

I let out a sound that was halfway between a grumble and a "what?" Blinking a few times, I realized it wasn't morning yet and pushed Frankie gently away then rolled back over and covered my head with my pillow.

"Go away," I mumbled.

"You gotta come with me." She pulled the pillow off my head and shook my shoulder gently.

"What are you talking about?" I asked, annoyed. Sleep was hard for me, and when I was finally able to get to sleep, being interrupted was a pain.

"I've gotta go check something out in the park."

Waking up enough to realize I probably needed to actually pay attention to whatever she was talking about, I rubbed my eyes and sat up. The red glow of the digital clock across the room read 1:47.

"Right now?" I shook my head. "The park is weird right now, and it's the middle of the night."

"Yeah, it won't take long."

Squinting in the small glow of her cell phone, I saw that she was fully dressed, wearing the same clothes she'd be in at school.

"Have you even slept yet?"

She shook her head. "I just need to check on something. Come with me."

"Ugh, fine." I was not at all interested in traipsing through the woods with her in the middle of the night. But I knew, in true Frankie fashion, she was going to go either way, and my anxiety was too high to let her go alone.

"Here." She tossed me a pair of leggings and a hoodie that I pulled over my pajama shorts and tank. She handed me a flashlight as I slipped on my boots.

This wasn't the first time we'd sneaked out at night, but usually I insisted on more elaborate plans to ensure we wouldn't get grounded afterward. This whole "hopping out of bed on a whim" situation had my nerves jangling, but the combination of worry for Frankie and also my mostly-still-groggy-from-sleep mind barely had me remembering to lock the doorknob.

I followed her out the bedroom window and onto the porch roof. We knew how to avoid popping the aluminum roofing with our weight and kept to the side of the small covering.

Frankie offered me her hand as we stepped down onto the wood-burning oven our moms had built out of bricks a few summers before, not realizing they were practically building a staircase for us to get off the roof.

Before I'd even hopped all the way down, Frankie was hurrying across the backyard to the fence that backed up to the stream running from our housing division to the park. We spent a lot of time exploring it during the summer months when we were younger, and now it was a good shortcut to our friends' houses.

We were almost to the turnoff for the park when I heard something rustling in the bushes beside me. I jumped, swinging my flashlight right into Meara's face.

"You scared the crap out of me!" I shrieked, and Frankie shushed me.

"Oh, Jean. Hi." Meara looked bemused.

"Hello to you too. What's going on?" I looked from Frankie to Meara. "Frankie didn't say you were meeting us."

"Same." Meara clicked on her own flashlight. Frankie was already ahead of us, and we shrugged, keeping up with her as best we could.

I lost sight of Frankie's flashlight and almost tripped over her when we reached the edge of the creek at the spot where a bridge crossed it. She was kneeling down next to the path, hunched over.

"Ouch!" I said. "What the heck, Frankie?"

But she tugged me down beside her and grabbed my flashlight, clicking it off before handing it back to me. "Shh. Listen."

Meara joined us.

It took a few minutes to slow my breathing enough to hear anything other than my own lungs pumping and for my eyes to adjust to the moonlight. It was slightly overcast, so there wasn't much to see by, but the moon peeked out from behind a slow-moving cloud.

"What are we listening for?" I asked quietly.

"I'll know it when I hear it." Frankie stared directly ahead. I realized she was staring at the same general area where Byron and I had seen the weird blob but from a different vantage point, though what she could possibly see in this dim light was beyond me.

I counted to one hundred in my head and still heard nothing out of the ordinary. No sounds other than an occasional small splash in the creek from a disturbed frog. A rustle of wings. The distant bark of a neighborhood dog.

"Come on, Frankie. There's nothing there. Let's go back," I whispered. My legs were cramping from hunching down, and I was already dreading the sound of my alarm going off in less than four hours.

Looking to Meara for agreement, I turned. But she wasn't there.

"Meara?" I whispered, looking in a circle around us. "Meara," I called again, louder this time.

"Shush," Frankie breathed.

"Where did she go?" I asked. I hadn't heard her move away. She couldn't have gone far. She had crouched down with us, right?

"I don't know, just shush," Frankie said, still quietly but harsher than usual.

"If y'all are playing a joke on me, I want you to stop right now."

Frankie sighed and looked at me, frustrated. "I need you to stay quiet."

"And I need you to tell me what you and Meara are doing." I was fed up. I stood and brushed off my knees. "I am too tired to deal with y'all pranking me."

"Meara?" Frankie asked, shaking her head.

"Yeah, Meara," I responded sarcastically. "About this tall and currently hiding somewhere, probably to jump out at me. I'm so annoyed with you both. I'm going back."

"Jean, wait." Frankie pulled at my hoodie sleeve. "Where did Meara go?"

"That's what I've been asking." Whatever was going on, I was tired of going along with it.

"Meara?" Frankie whispered, looking around for her like I had.

"I'm going home. This is annoying." I turned around and made my way back toward the mouth of the creek and toward our neighborhood.

"Wait, Jean. Don't go." Frankie hurried to catch up to me. "We have to find Meara."

I studied her face in the moonlight. She looked sincere.

"So, you two didn't plan something mean?" I asked.

Frankie shook her head earnestly and clicked on her flashlight. "I promise. I don't know where she is."

She swung her flashlight in a circle and called Meara's name again, still softy but more loudly than before. I did the same as we made our way back toward our houses.

"Meara, come out. This isn't funny anymore," I said. As we got closer to the neighborhood, I became equally bolder and angrier. I was worrying about her, and it was making me frustrated.

"Meara, where are you?" Frankie called.

"Do you have your cell phone?" I asked. We were close to the houses, and I didn't want to wake up any neighbors just because Meara was playing a random game of hide-and-seek.

"Yeah, one sec." Frankie stopped and flipped open her phone. Our parents were old school and insisted we have those indestructible Nokia phones that were just for calling and texting.

She pressed the seven for speed dial, and the sound of Meara's ringtone a second later just to our right made us both jump. I aimed my flashlight at the ringing cell phone, and Frankie did the same.

The phone was resting on a rock in the middle of the creek, the vibrations moving it closer to the edge of the moss covered stone.

"What?" Frankie asked just as Meara jumped at us from the bank.

We both screamed, and I dropped my flashlight with a splash into the water.

"Dang it, Meara. What the hell?" I pushed her away from me out of instinct as she laughed and pointed at us.

"You should see your faces," she cackled, flicking us both with water.

"That was not cool." I was definitely not getting enough sleep tonight. "You scared the crap out of me."

Meara kept laughing. And I let out a nervous chuckle.

I looked over where Frankie stood. She had said nothing since we had both screamed. Now, she was very still.

"Frankie?" I asked.

Meara was laughing so hard she was holding her belly.

"Why are you all wet?" Frankie asked Meara, eyes narrowed.

But Meara didn't answer. She just kept laughing like she was never going to stop, until I said loudly, "That's enough, Meara."

She sucked in a huge breath and went silent. Like someone had clicked mute on the television. Her hair was dripping wet, her clothes soaked as well. Her eyes went wide, and she started to shiver.

"Meara, are you okay?" I stepped toward her. But she waved me off. "Yeah, I'm just, I'm just..." She trailed off. "I need to get my phone."

"I'll get it for you," I volunteered. I reached for my flashlight, the glow visible a few feet below the water, but I hesitated and instead just used the cast-off light from Frankie's to step across a couple other rocks until I reached the one with her phone on it.

I hopped back, and she snatched it out of my hand, shivering.

Frankie hadn't moved.

"Okay, so let's all go home now, right?" I looked between the two of them. Something passed across Frankie's eyes as she stared at Meara, her hair stringy down the sides of her face, mud caking her fingers.

"Right," Frankie said, jerking her chin in the direction of Meara's house. "We'll see you tomorrow."

Meara wrapped her arms around herself and nodded, turning on her heel and disappearing into her backyard. We waited until we heard her backdoor open and shut before either of us spoke.

"I need my flashlight," I said, and stepped toward the water.

"Leave it," Frankie said. Her voice was even and firm. "I've got an extra you can have."

Chapter 11

I woke up the next morning more frustrated with my alarm than anything else. Out of pettiness, I didn't shake Frankie awake until after I was finished with a longer than usual shower using warmer than usual water.

But then I felt bad that she might be late and made her a cup of coffee while my tea brewed. I loved coffee as much as the next person, but on days I knew my anxiety was already going to be heightened from something—like, I dunno, an almost complete lack of sleep?—I liked to not add to it with excess caffeine.

"Hey, Frankie." I set her coffee on the shelf by her bed. Frankie had never been an early riser, but she was really conked out. "Frankie, come on. You're gonna be late."

Finally, she roused. "I'm sick. Tell Mom to call me in."

"She already left for work." I put my hand on Frankie's forehead since I was totally a medical professional. "Eww, you're all sweaty." I pulled my hand away and wiped it on my jeans.

"I told you." She rolled over, tugging the comforter over her head.

"I guess that a fever could explain your totally unhinged behavior last night." I pulled out my phone and called our mom.

75

"Hey, Mom." I filled her in. "Do you have any other symptoms?"

Frankie mumbled, "Just cramps."

"Just cramps," I relayed. Mom gave me a few more instructions, and I hung up. "She said get rest and she'll call you in to school and Ma's going to come home at lunch to check on you."

"Thanks," Frankie mumbled and went back to hiding under her covers.

I got ready for school and, before I left, set some Gatorade and a glass of water with some crackers and a bottle of ibuprofen on her nightstand shelf.

I thought she was asleep, but as I left, she poked her head out and said, "You're a really good sister, no matter what."

"You are too. Now get enough sleep for both of us. I'm still mad about whatever last night was." I gave Lucifer a scratch behind the ears where she was curled up at Frankie's feet. "Keep an eye on her for me while I'm gone, okay?"

I flipped off the light and closed the door behind me as I left the room.

"No Frankie today?" Byron asked as he pulled up alongside me on the walk to school.

"Nope, she's not feeling great."

His eyebrows knit together in worry. "I hope she's okay."

He looked backward down our street like she might pop out of the front door of our house anyway.

"We got, like, zero sleep, and she says she's having cramps, but I think that's just an excuse."

"I do not miss those at all." His parents and doctor had gotten him an IUD to stop his period a couple of years ago.

"She has been really weird lately. She dragged me out into the woods last night."

"What?" He frowned. "Why wasn't I invited?"

"Oh, that's what you're worried about?" I gave him a gentle push on the arm. "Trust me. It was not fun. We just looked into the darkness at something Frankie thought she saw, and then Meara scared the shit out of us both."

"Meara was invited?" Now, he was really feigning feeling left out.

"Listen, I had nothing to do with it, and Meara was all wet and acting super weird. Like, not fun weird."

"You don't think they're on drugs, do you?" he asked seriously.

"Who's on drugs?" Sam made me jump a little as he joined us.

"Dude, don't scare me," I scolded.

"I walk with you basically every single morning, Jean," Sam said. "Why are you so jumpy?"

"She was just filling me in on some weird middle-of-the-night excursion Frankie and Meara dragged her to," Byron said.

"And we weren't invited?" Sam whined.

"You two are ridiculous." I rolled my eyes. "No one was invited. I think it was a spur-of-the-moment thing. And no, I don't think they're on drugs. That seems more like a whole group activity?"

I could have been wrong. Frankie and I talked about trying some things out together eventually. Our parents were both really open about everything though, so my curiosity wasn't that piqued. Mom had even suggested I try out some CBD once I was old enough to apply for a license to see if it might help my anxiety.

But when Frankie had woken me up the night before, she hadn't seemed on anything. Just focused on finding whatever she'd been looking for. I still hadn't asked her for more details, but it seemed rude to press her on it since she woke up sick.

"So, what happened?" Sam asked.

I filled him in on what I'd told Byron then added the part about Meara jumping out at us and scaring the bejeezus out of me. "I'm not even ashamed. I almost peed my pants."

"They had to have planned it," Byron mused as we got up to the school.

"Well, if they did, it was mean," I said. "But I think Frankie was just as startled by Meara as I was."

"There's got to be something going on." Sam frowned. "Like how Mojito freaked out yesterday."

Byron nodded. "And whatever that weird blob we saw was."

"I just hope whatever is going on," I said, "it'll let me get a full night's sleep. I need my beauty rest, and Meara and Frankie have, alas, deprived me of such crucial REM."

"I'll give Meara a lot of grief first hour for you." Byron peeled off toward his homeroom.

"Please do," I called back as Sam and I headed to our first period.

Originally, I planned on spending my lunch period walking Frankie's schedule to pick up any assignments she might be missing and take them back home to her but turned out I didn't have to.

Sitting at our usual table, before anyone else had arrived, was Frankie.

Looking pale as a marble statue.

"Frankie, what are you doing out of bed?" I rushed over to her and sat down, instinctively putting my hand on her forehead, which was still hella clammy.

"I came to school." She shrugged.

"Yeah, but you're sick." Her almost completely shaved head somehow managed to look tousled, and her skin was flushed.

She pushed my hand away with a weak wave. "I'm fine."

I looked at her more closely. "You're wearing the same clothes as yesterday." I took in a breath. "And you stink. We need to get you home. Ma is going to freak out if she gets there to check on you and you're not in bed."

Without waiting for an answer, I put my hand under Frankie's elbow and helped her up. She gave a bit of a wobble as she stood. I had to take a breath and remind myself that she'd been out all night and was having cramps. Anytime she got even a little bit sick, the rest of us fussed, and it made her self-conscious and the rest of us anxious.

"I texted her," Frankie said.

"Who?" My mind had already jumped to worry and circled back.

"Our moms. I let them know I was going to school."

"Well, if they'd seen you, they would have told you to stay put. Come on. I'll walk you."

We checked out through the office, the administrative assistant not even hesitating to let us go when she caught sight of Frankie. I let her know I'd be back once I got her settled, but she assured me she'd checked me out for the day if I needed to take care of her and that she'd follow up with our moms. There were some benefits to living in a relatively small town and being involved in a bunch of extracurriculars and being the sister who never caused any trouble.

As I held Frankie's arm and we walked through the parking lot, she stumbled and would have fallen, but Lyla was there out of nowhere, grabbing her other elbow to steady her.

"Hey!" I said.

"Um, you doing okay there, Frankie?" Lyla asked.

Frankie gave Lyla the side-eye and pulled her arm back once she was standing upright again. "Never better."

"I'm walking her home." I nodded toward our house, which was almost in view but felt quite far away at the moment.

"I'll help," Lyla offered, and Frankie took her up on the re-offered elbow after she started to sway again.

"That is really nice of you, but don't you have to get to class?" I nodded toward the building behind us.

She shrugged. "I'm just getting here because I had an appointment and was kinda only coming to school for yearbook class, so I don't see the point. May as well tag along with you and make sure your sister makes it home in one piece."

At that, Frankie let out a loud noise that made me jump.

"Was that a sneeze?" I yelped. Sam was right—I really was jumpy right now. Maybe I needed sleep more than I thought.

Frankie nodded and wiped her arm on her sleeve.

"Come on. She looks like she needs a nap and maybe some medicine." Lyla took my backpack from me without my having to ask and slung it on next to hers. The three of us walked the rest of the way to our house, opting to go through the back gate since it was a bit shorter.

I sat Frankie, who seemed absolutely exhausted, down in a porch chair and left her with Lyla while I went around the front of the house to let us in.

We got Frankie up the stairs, and I got her undressed and into the bath, handing Lyla her clothes and thanking her when she offered to put them in the washing machine.

I tried not to think too hard about the fact that the first time Lyla was seeing my house was to help me get my sister taken care of like this, but I didn't hate the idea of her being in my house.

Until it occurred to me that she could very easily be going through my things. And she was probably looking at all the baby pictures on the walls.

But I didn't think someone who offered to wash someone else's sick sister's clothes would be in any way judgy about family photos? Plus, I was an exceedingly cute baby, an absolute butterball, so I wasn't sure what I was worried about.

Frankie was slowly washing her hair while I sat on the counter, and I was lost in thought when I heard her speak.

"What?"

And she mumbled again. I hopped off the counter and knelt down next to her so I could hear what she was saying.

"It's deep enough."

"What is?" I asked, not understanding.

"It's deep enough," she repeated.

"What is deep enough, Frankie?"

"The water."

"It's deep enough for what?"

"To take care of itself."

"Okay, we're getting you out." I leaned over to pull the plug, but Frankie grabbed my wrist. "Hey, cut it out."

"It's moving the wrong way."

"Frankie." I tried to jerk my hand away, but she held on tight. "Frankie, let go."

"You have to listen, Jean." She pulled me close and spoke directly into my ear. "The water. It's moving wrong."

Then, as suddenly as she had grabbed me, she let go and sat back, wiping her eyes. I plunged my hand in and pulled the plug, ready to get her out as quickly as I could.

"I'm so tired." She slumped to the side, resting on the edge of the tub. "Stay with me?"

Chapter 12

"Yeah, let's get you to bed." I was not a fan of this particular Frankie, who clearly needed to talk to her counselor—the therapist one, not the school one—about the incident with the skateboarders and the water and sooner rather than later. Maybe that was what had spurred the impromptu outing last night.

I helped her out of the tub and wrapped her in a giant towel. While she was brushing her teeth, I went to our bedroom to grab her some pajamas.

When I got there, Lyla was standing in the middle of a heap of bedsheets and jumped. "Sorry, I know it's presumptuous, but you said she'd slept in her clothes and I figured clean sheets would be good and I didn't have to dig around since they were right there in the laundry room."

I looked at the bunk bed and saw that both mattresses had been remade neatly.

"Thank you." I gave her a quick hug, startling us both a bit, but she hugged me back until I pulled away a moment later.

"I didn't know whose bed was whose right away, so I did the whole thing."

"Were you able to figure out which one was which?"

At this, Lyla blushed. Like, actually blushed. "I'm guessing yours is the one with all the pictures of cute, endangered animal

83

species and polaroids of your friends and, like, flowers and stuff? And Frankie's is the one with all the Ramones and Joan Jett magazine cutouts."

"Okay, yeah, I guess not that hard to figure out." I got into Frankie's dresser and pulled out a pair of sweatpants and a T-shirt. "I'll be right back. And thank you."

Lyla smiled, and I went back to the bathroom.

After knocking softly, I let myself in. Frankie was putting on some lotion, which I took as a good sign, and I helped her get into her pajamas. Then we walked down the hallway to our room.

When we got there, Lyla and the pile of dirty sheets were gone, the reading lamps were on, and the overhead light was off.

"Do you want to sleep on the bottom today?" I offered, but she shook her head.

Frankie hadn't touched her Gatorade or crackers yet, but she took a sip of water after I helped her climb up to the top bunk. She flopped down on the mattress, and I pulled the covers up.

"Let me know if you need anything." I left the room and pulled the door partway shut.

Lyla was sitting at the kitchen table with a cup of tea when I got there. When we were really little and Frankie was sick, we'd leave a little bell for her to ring when she needed us. I considered finding it but decided I'd most likely be hovering enough not to need it.

"Want some tea?" Lyla walked over to the counter to pull out a mug.

"That sounds great." I smiled and excused myself for a second to call my parents and give them an update on the Frankie situation.

"You're sure you can miss school this afternoon?" Mom asked, and I told her it was fine. I already knew what my assignments were, and I'd rather hang around and make sure Frankie was doing okay.

"You're a really good sister," she said.

"I know. I'm pretty much a totally really good person." I could see Lyla getting the tea box down from the cabinet. "Oh, also," I added, "um, I have a friend over, helping me out, so I hope that's okay?"

"Tell Byron we said hello," Mom guessed.

"Actually, it's not Byron. It's a new friend. Lyla."

There was a bit of a pause on the line. "Well, we look forward to meeting Lyla when we get home. At any moment."

I rolled my eyes, knowing they trusted me to make relatively good decisions, even though in the last few days I'd made a handful of questionable ones. Those were mostly Frankie's doing though.

"I love you both. Goodbye." I said into the phone as I pulled it away from my ear.

"We love you too." I heard my mom say as I hung up.

I walked back to the kitchen, and Lyla had the kettle on.

"I hope you don't mind. I went full Mrs. Doubtfire on your house just now." She smiled sheepishly.

"Not at all. You've been so freaking helpful. Thank you so much."

"My pleasure." She slid the mug across the counter, and I added some milk.

"You don't have to stay." But I wanted her to.

"I really don't mind. I enjoy snooping around your house." She grinned and made no move to leave, for which I was grateful.

"Mind if we go hang out in my room? I kinda want to keep an eye on Frankie?" I knew she was just up the stairs, but I was still worried about her.

"Yeah, sure," Lyla said. "Whatever you want, Jean."

I didn't mean to unload right then, but before I thought about it, I went on, "When we were little, Frankie got really sick."

"I'm sorry to hear that." Lyla waited for me to continue.

"Like, we didn't know if she was gonna survive, sick. My folks tried not to tell me much at first, but then they realized it was making me more anxious, not knowing what was going on. So, anyway. I try not to, but every time she gets sick at all, I get really freaked out. It drives her up the wall, but here we are."

Lyla reached a hand across the counter to cover mine.

"Thank you for telling me that." She gave my hand a squeeze, and her warm palm made me almost grateful that Frankie was sick, followed immediately by guilt. I really needed to talk to my own therapist soon.

"Come on." I grabbed a couple of bananas and some more tea, and we climbed up the stairs to our room.

On the way, Lyla asked, "How quiet do we need to be?"

"She's a pretty hard sleeper, so, like, whispering?"

Lyla nodded, and we went in. Listening for a minute, I could hear the sounds of Frankie breathing softly and steadily.

"I have an idea." Lyla sat down on the floor by my bunk bed. "Can I see your laptop?"

I took the computer from the charger and sat down next to her. She pulled up a web comic. "Have you read *Nimona?*"

I shook my head.

"Well, you are in for a treat." Lyla clicked on the first page, and the two of us sat together reading it, trying not to giggle too much at the funny parts. The faint glow from the laptop and the sunlight at the bottom of the curtains made it feel like a secret cave.

I must have dozed off because I woke up in my bed, a throw blanket covering me and Ma gently shaking me awake.

"Hey, we're home," she whispered.

"What time is it?" I asked.

"Just after four. I figured you wouldn't want to sleep through the whole afternoon." I nodded and sat up. Lyla had left, but I saw a note tucked under my closed laptop.

"Had to run, thanks for the tea. See ya tomorrow. — L"

I headed to the kitchen, where my folks were waiting for an update. There wasn't much to tell them other than Frankie seemed totally out of it and I was worried about her, which was my baseline. "She's been acting weird since we saved those kids."

They glanced at each other.

"We should probably both go see Ms. Duncan before too long."

"I'll email her now, sweetie."

"Thanks, Mom. I think I'm gonna see if Byron wants to study together, get out of the house for a bit." I pulled out my backpack and made sure the supplies I needed were in there.

"Okay, dinner at seven." Mom gave me a hug. "And what happened to your friend?"

"She had to go home, but I think you'll get to meet her soon, hopefully. She's really cool."

My parents smiled, and I headed out, shooting Byron a "come out and see me" text. I knew he'd be home by then and mostly just wanted to get out of my house and go over the wild afternoon with Frankie.

And maybe dish a little bit about Lyla.

By the time I got to his place, he'd made his way to the front yard with three bottles of lemonade, and Sam was there too, playing catch with Mo. The three of us stood around taking turns throwing the tennis ball for Mojito and going over what had happened the last few days.

"Meara wasn't at school at all today," Byron filled me in. "I went over and checked on her. Her mom said she was sleeping but that she was probably going to be back at school tomorrow, so that's good."

"Do you think it's going to get to all of us?" Sam tossed the ball at me, and I caught it then threw it for Mo. "Like if it's a virus?"

"Maybe." I didn't want to go back to distance learning, but this didn't really seem like that. If I didn't know Meara and Frankie as well as I did, I would probably guess they were on drugs. "I'm worried their teachers or our parents are gonna think they're on drugs."

Sam nodded. "I thought about that."

"I bet whatever it is clears up in no time. Maybe they actually are just having cramps." Byron threw the ball at Mo. "Last time, Mo. Then we have to go home."

I hadn't realized it was almost seven and I needed to get back. "I'll see you two tomorrow morning."

"See ya, Jean."

Giving Mojito one last scratch behind the ears, I walked back home, ready to eat some dinner and crash. Frankie was still asleep when I got there, and she stayed sleeping even when I went to bed.

The sun is bright, and you squint, shuffling your feet to the coolness of a shadow.

There is a thrum behind your eyes. It comes through the ground to your feet and into your legs.

One knee moves, and you're walking down a path that is invisible. But the direction is automatic.

"Shh. Shh."

A soothing voice comes from a murky cloud blocking your vision up ahead. You are unable to discern whether the sound is coming from the cloud or near it. Your feet propel you farther until you are wrapped in the fog. It is dark and cool against the harsh sunlight from before.

Chapter 13

"Good gravy, Jean. How many times have we told you that we will put up with pretty much anything except for egg salad?" Byron looked like he might actually throw up. But egg salad had always been my favorite, and if he was going to stop being my friend over one more lunch featuring it, so be it.

I took a bite with a shrug and mumbled, "I'll eat fast."

Byron rolled his eyes, and Sam shrugged, shoveling some pepperoni pizza into his mouth.

"I like egg salad," Lyla said, and I smiled at her, hoping that none of my lunch was in my teeth.

"Want half?" I offered, holding out half of my sandwich and inwardly dying of certainty that what I was doing was maybe the dorkiest thing I'd ever managed.

"Oh, sure," she said and took my sandwich. "You want half of mine?"

"Sure," I smiled and took her pimento cheese half.

I took a bite and smiled at her as she did the same.

Byron cleared his throat.

"What?" I asked, looking up. Everyone was staring at us with a variety of expressions, none of which were uninterested.

"Nothing," Byron started, looking between the two of us, "just glad everyone is eating sandwiches."

"You two aren't eating." Sam nodded to Frankie and Meara, who had an untouched container of soggy cafeteria fries between them.

"These fries are gross." Meara looked up at Sam and pushed the red-and-white-checkered boat of supposed food away and into the middle of the table.

"Yeah," Frankie said, pushing away the container of ketchup that was next to her. "I'm not starving."

"Didn't you skip breakfast?" I asked, worry suddenly ruining the fun of the sandwich swap.

Frankie shot me a look that gave very "you're way too concerned, sis," vibes. So, I took another bite of sandwich, but I kept eye contact so she knew I was only dropping it because I'm respectful. It was only yesterday that she'd been laid up in bed.

Also, Lyla's sandwich was freaking great.

"What did you do to this?" I asked through a bite.

Lyla grinned. "I can't tell you. It's a family secret. Passed down from generation to generation."

Then she winked at me, and I was suddenly super not great at chewing for a second.

"Y'all are weird about your sandwiches." Frankie crossed her arms and looked at us. But I just shrugged and took another bite.

Toward the end of lunch, I met up with Blakely and Jack. The second river cleanup of the year was coming up sooner than we had originally planned because both of them were eager to keep the momentum going.

"Everyone is paying attention to the eco kids right now. It's a good time to drum up enrollment," Jack was saying.

"It's not weird to you that we're capitalizing on two kids almost drowning?" I asked, somewhat bothered by the number of people who were suddenly interested in the environment. Not that it was a bad thing. I'd just spent the last four years feeling like I had to guilt my friends and family into showing up to make sure at least someone was there and now there were dozens of people saying they would come.

"The kids are fine, right? So, no harm." Jack shrugged and added to the list we were making of supplies to pick up.

"It's more important now than ever since those kids could have been hurt really bad," Blakely pointed out as she went over the checklist. "We need to make sure this cleanup happens. What if they'd hit, like, metal garbage or something?"

We'd decided to have everyone bring their own bags and gloves to save money, but there was still enough in the budget to provide some coffee and pastries.

"I guess that makes sense." But I still had a bit of a knot in my stomach about going back out there so quickly after the incident.

"You look worried." Jack gave me a pat on the shoulder. It was in a very "older brother who knows better" way, but at least he was being kind.

"Mrs. Carson wants everyone who comes to wear a safety vest." I pulled out the box that she'd slid into the closet at the back of the biology classroom. Inside were fifty reflective orange vests.

"Well, there goes trying to be cool," Jack said sarcastically. "I thought we were trying to not be total dorks."

"Shut up, dude. Saving the environment is what makes us cool. Well, that and varsity basketball," Blakely said, grabbing one and pulling it over her head. The girl looked like Captain Marvel half the time, and I wondered absently if she would use her powers for good. We'd known each other since middle school but hadn't exactly been friends that whole time. "This is a good idea."

Jack shrugged. "Whatever."

I rolled my eyes, ready to get this meeting over with and meet up with Lyla. "Okay, so I'll see you guys bright and early on Saturday?"

They both nodded.

I tried in vain to focus on my afternoon classes, and not worry about what felt like such a tiny dent we were making on the cleanup. If I thought about it too hard, it felt hopeless. The Stonefish Creek Nature Park was such an important part of the environment in our town, and it was constantly getting trashed. Eventually though, the day wrapped up.

"Ready?" Frankie stood up from the curb in front of the school where she'd been sitting reading a book and slung on her backpack while I gave Meara a hand up.

"Yep. Sam's coming too." I nodded toward the door of the school, and sure enough, he was right on time, Byron in tow.

"What were y'all doing?" Meara asked as we all turned to walk home.

"NHS hours shelving stuff in the library." Byron held out his fingers. "I swear I have gotten, like, seventeen paper cuts."

"Are you throwing the books like a frisbee?" Frankie asked, examining his fingers like they held some secret.

"I'm just a really enthusiastic future librarian." He laughed, and we cut across the field. The weather was perfect. I could almost smell fall, even though Frankie insisted I was jumping the gun on it and needed to lower my expectations of October in Oklahoma.

Which, true, but a girl could dream.

I couldn't wait until the leaves changed colors. For about five days, our walk home would be a rainbow between the green of summer and the barenness of winter.

"So, how was your afternoon? Enjoy any quality time with the new yearbook editor?" Sam waggled his eyebrows, and I groaned. "That fun, huh?"

I pushed him lightly, and those familiar butterflies started doing the cha-cha slide. "Yes, Sam. The whole staff is top-notch this year. So grateful to have them on my team."

I wasn't going to make this easy for him. I loved my friends, but I swore I was telling none of them about any crush I ever got in the future and had told them as much.

"Any plans for the weekend?" Byron asked once the jokes about me and Lyla had petered out.

"Just the second cleanup." I nodded toward the creek side of the nature park. "Can y'all make this one too?"

Everyone nodded, along with slightly grumbled demands for baked goods and coffee to be provided in some form.

"Is that it?" Byron asked. He, Sam, and I all looked at Meara and Frankie.

They glanced between each other and then shrugged at the same time.

"Why are you asking us?" Frankie held eye contact with Meara as she asked.

"Um because you two are the ones who always tell us what we're going to do?" Sam pointed out as though it was the most obvious thing in the world, though Frankie and Meara didn't seem to think so.

"Right." Meara kept walking. "No plans yet."

"You two are being weird. Are you being weird?" Byron crossed his arms and raised an eyebrow.

"We're not being weird." Meara spread her hands out, as if showing us that she was not physically holding weird.

"Anyway, we need to get moving if we're gonna have time to eat before our study session," Byron pointed out, and the two of us headed home.

"We have no such important tasks, so we're gonna go play with Sam's dog," Frankie said.

Sam frowned. "Um, am I invited to this hang out?"

Meara barked out a laugh. "Only if you keep your hands to yourself and let us get all the pets."

"Okay, fine," he said. "But even if Mojito ignores me when you're both around, she still loves me. As long as we remember that."

Frankie waved her hand dismissively. "Everyone knows I'm your dog's favorite."

I gave Sam a pat on the shoulder. "It's okay, buddy. We can't all be Mo's favorite."

"I'm just saying, I have to pick up the poops," he said. "That has to count for something."

Our two groups peeled off with a wave, and as Byron and I took the back gate into my house, I could still hear Sam arguing that having to give his dog a bath should make him higher on the favorites list.

Chapter 14

There was a note on the counter from our folks, letting me know they'd be at a work dinner and to help ourselves to leftovers and snacks.

"Okie charcuterie?" I asked, and Byron gave me a thumbs-up. So we started pulling everything we considered even remotely snack worthy out of the fridge and pantry and onto the counter.

"We doing a theme?" Byron held up two jars of pickles.

"Rainbow?" I suggested even though we'd done rainbow, like, five times in a row. It was the best way though.

"Works for me." We spent the next fifteen minutes arranging bites of food across a giant cutting board in a relatively coherent rainbow color scheme. When we finished, our masterpiece included strawberries for red, a whole banana for yellow, and one singular Zoloft for the blue as a joke because we couldn't find anything that color and it was time for my afternoon meds anyway.

We each grabbed a seltzer and plopped down at the dining room table to dig into our calculus homework.

Before I knew it, the front door was opening, and the tray of food was nothing but crumbs and a couple of browning apple slices.

I hadn't realized how much time had passed and assumed it was Frankie coming in, so it surprised me when I saw it was my folks home from their dinner. Glancing at the clock for the first time in ages, I realized it was almost nine.

"Hey, you two," my parents said and gave us each a side hug.

"Hey. How was your dinner?" Byron stretched and cleared off the table with me as we packed up our textbooks and notes.

"It was lovely." Mom smiled. I really hoped I got a job I'd enjoy as much as she enjoyed hers. "And how was studying?"

"Good." I was glad we'd done the session. "There were a couple of concepts that were kicking my butt. It felt good to sort them out."

"You helped me just as much as I helped you." Byron pointed his protractor at me menacingly.

"True but mostly by providing the fuel we needed."

"That is just as important," Byron insisted. "Brain food."

"Well, we're proud of both of you." Ma poured a glass of water and excused herself. "I'm going to go say hey to Frankie."

"Oh." I stood up. "She's not home yet, but she and Meara are just at Sam's. I'll walk Byron home and get her."

"Perfect," Mom said. "Be safe. We'll see you in a bit."

"You ready?" I asked, and Byron nodded, grabbing his backpack and telling my folks thanks again.

"You're always welcome here, Byron," Mom said. "Always."

"I know." He blushed warmly as we walked out the front door. My moms were some of the first grownups Byron had told he was trans after he'd told his own folks. They always made sure he knew how welcome he was.

"Do you think they're at his house or the park?" I asked as we headed down the street. Byron's house was close to Sam's, and I hoped that's where they were because I was wiped out now that I'd finished the cramming.

"We can try his house first," Byron suggested.

"You don't have to go with me. You can just head home if you want."

"Nah," he insisted. "Can't have you getting snatched up by the big bad wolf."

"You listen to too much true crime."

"I'm hooked. What can I say?"

"I guess it could be worse. You could be addicted to drugs or, like, something I don't care about at all."

Byron laughed. "I like how drugs and me liking something you don't are equally appalling to you."

"You know what I mean." I chuckled. "It's much easier to support you when you're writing weird short fiction I want to read."

We walked the rest of the way down the street to Sam's house.

When we got closer, we could hear the sound of Sam and Mojito in the backyard, so we popped our heads in the gate. They had six-foot privacy fences but always left the side gate unlocked.

"Hey, Sam, it's us," I semi-yelled. I didn't want to be too loud in case Henry might be asleep, though his room was on the other side of the house and upstairs so I wasn't too worried.

"Come on back," he yelled, and that was when we heard him talking to his dog in firm and soothing tones. "Stop it, buddy," Sam was saying. "What are you doing? Hey, hey, calm down."

When he came into view, his usually puddle-of-sappy-love dog was straight-up baring her teeth. Hackles raised along her back, the dog was salivating in a super gross way and crouched down, eyes wide and unblinking, tail tucked between her legs. The low rumble in Mojito's chest was frightening.

I expected to see some sort of mountain lion in the shadows, so it was quite disconcerting when, standing at the back of the yard, backs to the fence, I saw both Meara and Frankie.

"What's going on?" Byron looked between the four of them.

"Mojito, stop. Shh, it's okay. You know them. Hey. Hey," Sam kept repeating, his hand firmly on the collar around Mo's neck.

I didn't know what to do. I took a step toward Frankie and Meara, and Mo lunged to the left, dragging Sam with him so she was now standing between me, Byron, and Sam and the other two girls.

"Frankie, just climb the back fence," I said as calmly as I could. I didn't want to startle Mojito. I couldn't imagine something setting her off enough that she might bite someone. That would suck so much.

But Frankie didn't respond. She barely moved. Her eyes were blank and staring at the space where the dog had been a few seconds before.

"Meara," I tried. "Just climb the back fence. What are you doing?"

"They're not answering me," Sam sputtered between soothing commands at Mo that were clearly not working.

I took another step to get around the dog, but there was no moving her.

"Frankie!" This time I yelled.

She tilted her head and looked at me.

"Frankie Grace Harlow!" I yelled again.

This time, she shook her head in a shuddering movement. Her eyes went wide at the dog, and her jaw dropped. She looked at me with a question in her eyes.

"The fence," I pleaded. "Frankie, climb the damn fence."

From across the yard, we saw her grab Meara's shoulder and give it a shake. Then the two of them turned and scrambled quickly over the six-foot fence, landing on the other side with a thump.

As soon as they were out of sight, it was like a light switch had gone off, and suddenly Mo was chill again. Her tail wagged, and she looked over at me and Byron like she was seeing us for the first time. Mojito jumped over and turned around so I could scratch her butt where she always got me to.

"What the hell?" Byron asked.

"You two okay?" I called over the fence.

It took a beat or two before Meara called back, "Yeah, we're good."

"I'll see you at home," Frankie shouted.

"What happened?" I asked Sam, who stood and brushed dirt off his pants. He was shaking.

"I have no idea. She's never like that." Sam sat on a lawn chair, and Mo laid her head on his lap like always. "I feel so bad. She's usually so nice to everyone and she's being so weird lately."

"We know that," Byron reassured him. "Maybe something set her off. Was there, like, a cat around or something?"

Sam shook his head. "We were all just hanging out, and then maybe five minutes ago, she just lost her mind like she did the other day in the park."

"What were they doing?" I asked, giving Mojito another scratch. She was totally back to her normal loopy self.

"Literally the same thing we'd been doing all afternoon. Taking turns throwing her ball and talking about, like, anime and stuff."

"Strange." I looked around the yard, wondering if we could see what had gotten her so riled, but whatever it was must have been to do with Meara and Frankie.

"I feel terrible. She's seriously never this bad. I think we need to take her to the vet to make sure she's okay." Sam looked near tears, and I didn't blame him. One reason I didn't want to get a dog was the responsibility. I knew what might happen if someone got bit really bad. One of the worst things I can imagine.

"Hey, it was just a weird thing." I gave Mojito another pat. "She's a good doggo, aren't you?"

And as if showing off, she wagged her tail even harder and let her tongue wag out.

"I'm sure Meara and Frankie aren't going to hold it against either of you," Byron added. "They both love Mo to death."

We said our goodbyes and headed the half block home.

"That was wild," I stated the obvious as we got to Byron's driveway.

"Just glad no one was hurt."

"Yeah, me too."

"I'll see you in the morning, Jean."

"Night, Byron."

I walked the last few houses home a bit more quickly than I might have usually.

Chapter 15

Frankie beat me home and was already in her bunk when I came in.

"Hey, are you okay?" I started changing into pajamas, and when she didn't respond right away, I tossed a pair of socks at her.

"Eww, gross." She batted them aside and sat up.

"I asked if you were okay."

She nodded slowly. "Yeah, I'm fine."

"Well, that was freaking weird, wasn't it?" I grabbed my water bottle to fill it up when I went to brush my teeth.

"What was?" She frowned slightly.

"Mojito flipping out at you two?" I cocked an eyebrow at her.

"Oh, yeah. That was weird."

I crossed my arms and grabbed a towel, deciding I would shower even though it was late. I wanted to cool off from the study session and the weird incident with Mo. "Yeah, it was. Do you know what happened that got her so riled?"

She shook her head slowly.

I rolled my eyes. "Right, well, I'm going to go take a shower."

"Isn't it really late?" Frankie looked out the window like it would tell us the time, absently petting Lucifer, who was curled on her pillow.

"Yeah, so?" I was trying to shower in the evenings more, rather than the mornings, which was never a good idea because I was constantly worried that I would be late for homeroom. Something which had happened exactly twice and both times were excused.

Let the thought in.

Let it out.

Frankie knew that.

"No reason." She laid down. "Turn the light out when you go, please."

"Sure thing. Night, sis."

"Night."

I turned off the light but left my bedside lamp on so I could see when I got back.

Unfortunately, when I went to turn on the shower, instead of draining, it puddled in the bottom of the tub. I let out an audible groan and called down the hallway to my folks.

I could see their light was on, leaving a glow underneath their door jamb, so I waited a beat before I called again.

"Mom, the drain is clogged,"

But I really wanted to get in a quick shower, and they might have been reading and not heard me. I'd slept hella hot the night before and woken up sweaty enough that I had changed my sheets when I got up, and even though maths wasn't exactly the most dramatic of tasks, I still wanted to rinse the day off.

When my hollering elicited zero response from anyone in the house, I decided I'd try to see what was clogging the drain.

Taking an old toothbrush from the bucket of cleaning supplies under the sink, I bent over and stabbed it into the drain in a very technical way. There was definitely something clogging it.

I was essentially a plumber now.

Grimacing, I reached my fingers in and pinched what I could. It felt like a piece of cloth. Maybe someone had somehow managed to lose a tampon? Was that a thing that happened?

It took a second try, but I twisted and pulled, and it came loose.

Between my fingers was a clump of hair that just kept coming and coming, black and oily. I kept pulling it until I had what felt like an entire wig's worth of stringy, knotted tresses.

Then with a pop, the mass came loose from the pipe, and a gust of one of the worst things I have ever smelled in my life came through right as I screamed, flinging the cat-sized chunk against the mirror.

I gagged on the smell and hurried to open the small window and turn on the bathroom vent to air it out.

Coughing into the hall, I bumped into Ma, who had come to see what the screaming was about, just as the fire alarm began blaring.

I put my hands up to my ears, startled by the sound.

"What's going on?" she asked.

"There was something in the drain." I coughed. I noticed Frankie standing in our doorway, mouth open slightly, looking at my quizzically. "I pulled it out."

I turned back toward where the glob had landed against the mirror, just in time to see it slide into the bathroom sink, fitting down the drain as though it was made purely of water and not thousands of strands of hair.

"Why is the fire alarm going off?" Ma asked, and I shrugged.

I realized where the alarm was coming from. "Wait, it's the carbon monoxide detector."

But then it shut off as quickly as it had begun blaring.

"Can a bad smell set those things off?" I asked, stepping back into the bathroom, where most of the stench seemed to have dissipated.

There was no sign of the glob that had landed in the sink. What was going on?

My mom came in and inspected the drain, turning the water on in the tub. The drain ran perfectly.

"Well, whatever you did, maybe we can cancel the plumber." She shrugged and turned the water off. Then she looked at her watch and at me. "You better get to bed, love. It's late."

I skipped the shower and turned on my laptop to research if a smell could set off a carbon monoxide detector. The answer was yes, but it made me wonder how many chemical particles had gotten into my lungs for them to set off the alarm.

And what in the world was in our pipes?

And why did it look so much like that thing Byron and I had found in the park?

While I was on my laptop, I checked my email and had one from someone I didn't recognize. I clicked to open it.

Hello, I got your email address from the ambulance driver the other day and forgot about it until now. I was wondering if you knew anything about what happened to Aedan and Brantly when they got hurt. They've been acting really weird, and I don't know if something else happened. Anyway, sorry to bother you. We're really grateful you were there. If you could email us back, that would be good.

Brandi (Aedan's mom)

I quickly typed out a reply asking her to clarify what she meant by weird and hit send then threw on some pajamas and ran a comb through my hair, hoping that dry shampoo would make it at least tolerable in the morning.

Apparently, baseball caps were going to be my thing this semester.

I tried to lie down and close my eyes. But every noise was keeping me up, and I wasn't sure if my folks would be annoyed if I resubscribed to the app I sometimes used to help me fall asleep.

Frankie was sleeping above me. Her quiet breathing was steady, and I hoped she wouldn't have any nightmares. I was already grievously lacking sleep.

I texted Byron on the off chance he still was up too, but no luck after a few minutes. I wanted to tell him about the goop in person, so I shot him a "For real call me anytime" text.

Eventually, I was going to have to shower. There was just no way around it. I briefly considered using the showers at the school gym. But I was having a hard time getting that smell out of my head, so I went and opened our windows as far as I could.

Lucifer must have heard them open because she appeared on one of the window ledges and immediately nudged me with her head until I gave her the proper number—fourteen—of pets.

I grabbed my book for English class, hopeful Hemingway would put me to sleep. But three chapters in and I was beginning to wonder if I should let my therapist know about this apparent insomnia I was experiencing.

My laptop dinged quietly, and I saw that the kid's mom had already messaged me back. I opened up the email and read it quickly.

> *Neither of them has been eating much, and Aedan has started sleepwalking. We're worried he might be having some anxiety or something. Or maybe he got a bug during the accident. Just wanted to check and see how you all were doing.*

That was nice of her to check on us. I didn't want to send too much info about Frankie, though those symptoms were like what she and Meara were having, minus the sleepwalking as far as I knew.

Maybe there was some sort of bacteria in the water.

I wrote back a quick "Thanks for letting me know. I'll be in touch if I find anything out," and shut my laptop.

You wake up on the ground. The taste of mud is thick and gritty in your mouth. You push the dirt across your teeth with your tongue, which feels too heavy.

Everything is dark except for the light at the end of a tunnel.

You are underground. Sitting up, you spread your arms wide and touch both sides of the walls. They are round and metal. You realize you're in a pipe. The pipe feels familiar. You have been here before. It might be best to leave. But another thought is louder, and you turn toward the back of the pipe and, crouching, make your way farther in. Away from the small pinpoint of light.

Palms scrape against gravel and bits of stones and fish bones as you crawl toward the hole in the wall. You've been in that hole before. You hesitate. You don't want to go back inside the hole. A whistle in your ear. Wind against a bolder. Bracing your hands against the opening, you crawl inside.

Chapter 16

Sleep continued to elude me so I switched to my history textbook and read about the Silk Road until I must have drifted off because I woke up the next morning to Frankie trying to slowly take the textbook out from under my face.

"Sorry I woke you up," she whispered. "But you were drooling on the questions for chapter seventeen. Sleep tight, sis."

She clicked off the lamp by my bed, and I fell back asleep for what felt like twelve seconds before my alarm was blaring.

I moaned and threw my arm over my eyes. I was suddenly not prepared to face the day. I got up, and the first thing I noticed was just how ratty my hair felt. I groaned but decided to get a cup of tea before untangling it. Glancing at the clock on my bedside, I realized it was almost time to leave for school.

"Messy bun and a baseball cap, it is." I rolled out of bed and popped up to see if Frankie was awake.

She was not, so I gave her a shake.

"Mmhmm," she mumbled.

"Frankie, we have to go to school."

She groaned and threw her pillow at me. I swatted it away but not before I noticed the streaks of red and brown across it.

"Frankie? Is that blood?" I asked, picking it up and realizing I was right. "What happened? Are you okay?"

Letting out another groan, she sat up and gave me a very annoyed look.

"What are you talking about?" Frankie asked, and I shook her pillow at her.

Rubbing her eyes, she winced, a confused look on her face.

"What happened?" I repeated.

She held her hands out to me, palms up. Each had gashes along the center and across her fingers. Places where she'd already been scraped had re-opened. She looked at me, confusion on her face. "I don't know."

"How can you not know?"

Frankie shrugged.

"Well, I'll go get moms."

But she grabbed my arm quickly. "No, they'll both just worry. I'll clean them up. Maybe I just petted Luce one too many times and she got onto me about it."

Lucifer was known to assert her boundaries from time to time, but usually Frankie and I could tell when it was about to be a thing.

But it gave me pause, remembering the email about the skateboarders and sleepwalking. Though I would have woken up if Frankie had been walking around our room. I was sure I'd have worry lines on my face permanently by the time I was nineteen.

"Fine but let me help you." I was going to be worried all day about her getting an infection if I didn't make sure she cleaned her hands up properly.

Shuffling to the bathroom, I multi-tasked, brushing my teeth while rummaging around for the first aid supplies. If anyone was more prone to sleepwalking, it was me. I was constantly babbling about nonsense, and I knew that people who talked in their sleep were more likely to do other active things.

I spit and pulled my hair into what was essentially a bird's nest then went back to our room where Frankie was pulling on a fresh pair of ripped jeans and a baggie Nirvana T-shirt.

"Over here," I said, and Frankie sat on the edge of my bed.

"Do you know what you're doing?" she asked as I set out peroxide, gauze, and some Neosporin.

"I got literally the highest badge for first aid in scouts."

"You quit scouts when you were ten." Frankie winced as I uncapped the peroxide and poured it across the jagged scrapes, thoughts of bacteria invading my hamster wheel of a brain.

"Yeah, well, you know that there isn't all that much to it. It's not like they revoke your badges when you quit. I know to stop the bleeding, sanitize, etc." I wrapped her hands in the gauze as gently as I could, trying not to focus on the wounds underneath the bandages when I was done. "I would really like it if you told me what happened."

"I just really suck at skateboarding." Frankie stood and shrugged on a hoodie, even though it was plenty warm out.

"You just said it was Lucifer."

I could tell she was being evasive, and I didn't know why. But it was almost time for school, and I was planning on meeting up with Lyla to finish printing the film we'd developed.

Thinking about her gave my tummy a little flip, which I promptly took for nerves about my first hour quiz.

We waved goodbye and hustled out the door, catching the muffins our parents tossed us as we went.

"That's the most wholesome display of parental love that I've ever seen," Meara said, as we handed her an extra muffin, and headed to school, catching up with the others as we went.

Byron was the only one who asked about Frankie's hands, and she just shrugged and said the same thing to him that she had to me. It still didn't feel right.

Later during passing periods, I asked Meara about it. "When was the last time you two went skateboarding?"

Meara cocked her head and didn't respond immediately. "Why? Did she say something?"

"Just that she hurt herself skating," I replied, grabbing my math book and math pencil bag. Yes, I had multiple pencil bags. Math required an entirely different set of tools. Why would anyone mix them with the color-coding highlighters required for such subjects as US History and English Literature?

Meara still hadn't responded, but when I turned toward her and closed my locker, she had a blank look on her face, like she hadn't heard me at all.

"Hello, Meara, did you hear me?" I waved my hand in front of her face.

She blinked slowly then shook her head. "Sorry, I zoned out. What were you asking?"

"When was the last time you and Frankie went skateboarding?" I spun the combination lock, and we walked toward class.

"Oh, I'm not sure."

This gave me pause, but I didn't want to rat Frankie out for whatever she was hiding. Especially since I had no idea what it was. But now Meara was acting odd, and my anxiety was quickly gaining ground.

"Never mind." If they wanted to be vague and weird, that was up to them. It wasn't my business.

Which was a logical thought I had, immediately followed by that anxious hollow feeling I always got any time I felt like Frankie was excluding me. I was constantly worried she was hiding some clue she had about her own body that might indicate she was sick again. My therapist said that sort of anxiety was typical for people whose sibling had gone through a near-death type of sickness, and it was something I was pretty sure I'd never be able to shake.

So, it didn't help that Frankie practically ignored me all the times we were in classes together. She kept laying her head down, which was stressing me out even more.

I was grateful that we were on block scheduling though, so the whole second half of the afternoon would be in yearbook. When I got there, Lyla was already working on some spreads, and I took my regular computer next to her.

"Hey, how are you?" I asked.

She beamed at me and moved her backpack from where she'd placed it on the seat I was going to use. "I'm good. How are you?"

I wasn't planning on being honest with that quite standard greeting, but I spilled a lot in the two minutes before Mrs. Camp came in and started class.

"Wow," she said, "you really don't like it when your sister acts weird."

"I mean, it's not really just that. Like, she's weird all the time. That's sort of her vibe. But she doesn't usually leave me out of the weirdness."

Lyla placed a hand over mine and gave it a squeeze. "I'm sure she'll talk to you about it when she's ready. And it may not even be anything big. She's probably worried about college admissions or something."

This made me laugh. "Frankie is definitely not going to college after we graduate."

"Oh, sorry, I just assumed."

"It's okay, she just has some very solid ideas about brain development, the ivory tower concept, privatization of education." I ticked off Frankie's talking points.

"Wow, so she's thought it through."

"Yeah, I finally made a whole PowerPoint presentation for her to present to our moms after the counselors approached them about her not going to college. Though some people are holdouts that won't accept it."

"What about you?" Lyla asked as we clicked away at the layouts we were wrapping up before our first quarter deadline.

"I'm definitely planning to go, but I'm going to get my general ed credits out of the way and live at home for at least a year. Maybe two. My folks said they'd help me pay for state school all four years. But I like the idea of being around Frankie, and I can finish my degree on time anyway."

Lyla smiled at me. "Sounds like you have it all planned out. What are you going to study? Photography?"

I laughed at this. "No, environmental engineering. I want to save the planet, remember?"

"Oh, right, you might have mentioned that once or twice." She laughed, and the sound almost sent me into a full gay panic. How did anyone get anything done ever?

But somehow, I managed and with more than half the class block to spare. With the teacher's permission, Lyla, me, and two art students who were working on their own photography projects made our way into the darkroom.

The film we'd developed the other day was ready to look through, and we took it over to the light table before we flipped the lights to the red so we could decide which of the images to enlarge onto paper. While we had free rein of any supplies that remained from years past, we didn't want to do the whole roll because it would take ages and also photo paper was expensive and I didn't want to have to save up for more.

"So how should we pick this time?" Lyla asked, spreading out the strips of film and squinting. I handed her a magnifying glass, and we each took half of the negatives. "For this round, just pick the ones that stick out as the most interesting to you. We'll go from there."

"Sounds good."

We spent a few quiet minutes looking through them.

"I think this one of Meara and Frankie will be cool," she said, "but the side seems sort of blurry like before. Maybe it's a problem with the camera and not how we developed it?"

"Let me see." I leaned over, and when Lyla didn't lean away, I had to remind myself to breathe. Which was becoming an annoying habit and if I was going to take myself seriously and not just melt into a blobby gay puddle, I needed to get it together.

She was right. It looked like a smudge next to the two of them, but until we enlarged it, there was not a good way to tell what exactly was making the distortion.

"Let's do that one and see what's up with the blurry part. And I like these two." I'd marked several with clips so we could find them.

Once the art students had theirs sorted out, we flipped off the lights and turned on the "photo development in progress" sign outside the door.

As the images transferred onto the paper, we took turns going through the steps. Hanging them up on the line to dry was the last one, and both Lyla and I stood looking at the images we'd chosen.

"Maybe there is something wrong with my camera after all," I said. There were definitely portions of the images that made no sense.

"Whoa, how did you do that?" one junior asked.

I shrugged. "I have no idea. It wasn't on purpose."

Like the photo of them in the pipe, this one had a portion that looked burned. They were sitting on the curb in front of our house, and the edges of the photo made a squiggly frame. What looked almost like tendrils of hair seemed to be pushing through the air in the gap between them and the edges.

I blinked, and it looked more like a blur again. Sort of like those magic eye paintings. When you softened your vision just right, you could see something that wasn't there before.

"Do you see that?" Lyla asked softly, staring at the same image as I was.

"You mean the giant wig coming out of the side of the photo?"

"Yeah, that."

I nodded. "Yeah, I see it."

"What the hell is it?"

"I have no idea."

Chapter 17

"You all stay safe today," Mom said as Byron and I loaded up the truck bed with the supplies for the stream cleanup.

Blakely and Jack had done the hardware store run, so we had all the trash bags and gloves we thought we'd need since so many extra students had signed up for the activity.

"I really don't like how excited everyone is about this because two kids almost drowned." I was grumpy. Frankie had slept in instead of trekking out there with us, which was her decision, but I was still bummed she wouldn't be there.

Meara, Lyla, and Sam were going to meet us any minute though, so I did my best to shake it off.

Byron was finishing up matching up sets of work gloves. "Whatever the reason, just focus on the fact that the creek is gonna get cleaned up, which is very much needed."

"That's true." I was still feeling squeamish about the blob situation and whatever that smell had been. Anxiety about the incident with those two kids wasn't lost on my brain either. I needed something to focus on other than the stress of the previous cleanup and all the other weird stuff that had been going on.

"And didn't you say you want to take another roll of film, since something went wonky with the last two?" Byron added.

I nodded. I was still not sure what had caused the weird results on the photos we'd developed, though it could have been just about anything. I planned to run another roll through and develop those, so if I did need to take my camera into the repair shop near my house, I would have some examples to help them figure out what might be causing it. I'd also borrowed Ma's old point-and-shoot to try a few with that and see if it made a difference. A quick internet dive had pointed me toward possible light leaks, but I wasn't sure. Some of the images were so delightfully clear and crisp. I should have realized that darkroom photography was as much science as art.

The others showed up around that time, and we piled into the truck.

"I brought donuts." Lyla cheerfully held open the box as soon as she buckled up next to me on the bench seat.

"Oh, thank you." Sam plucked a chocolate glazed one out of the box.

I glanced at it but shook my head. None of them looked particularly tempting.

"What about…" Lyla paused dramatically then produced a cinnamon twist from behind her back. "This?"

The grin exploded on my face, and I took the donut, my favorite, from her.

"Thank you!" I took a huge bite. It was still warm, and I didn't care that cinnamon and sugar were going to be all over me. We'd be knee deep in trash soon enough.

I think maybe she was blushing, and Sam and Byron were giving each other a look that I caught in the rearview mirror.

"Anyone else?" Lyla offered the box out the truck window, and Byron took a sprinkle one. Meara shook her head. I took the last couple of bites of mine, followed by a drink of iced tea.

Clearing my throat, I said, "Okay, let's do this."

Meara, Lyla, and I rode in the truck, followed by Byron and Sam on bikes.

The turnout was even more than we had guessed. Apparently, a bunch of people brought friends with them, so we wound up with about fifty people.

"Huge shout out to everyone who came today." Blakely was standing on the tailgate, doing the announcements that I usually took care of because the thought of speaking in front of that huge number of people made me want to vomit. She ran through the instructions, including the safety ones, though we ran out of the orange vests so decided to just make sure that at least everyone had a buddy with one on.

There were a few extra sponsors with us this time as well, though they seemed equally as engaged with each other as they were with students. I was just glad that, if anything did happen, we wouldn't have to be in charge.

"How about we go the other direction this time?" Sam suggested, and we all agreed, making our way across the field to the entrance of the park and crossing over the large wooden bridge on the northern edge.

Pointing down to the bottom of the creek that the bridge extended over, Byron suggested, "Let's go down the lower part and work our way up here from there. We can circle back and do the other side afterward."

We peeled off the path to walk about the length of a football field downward to where this part of the water reached the swampy embankment. We weren't the only ones with the idea, and when we got to the bottom, Blakely's group was starting on the other side.

"Hey!" I called, and they waved. At this part, we were maybe twenty feet away. But the water would peter out, and we'd all be side by side once we made our way upstream.

It took time though.

The garbage in this area was badly tangled. We took turns pulling at branches and tossing them up the bank so we could separate the garbage from the undergrowth.

Plastic bags were wrapped around logs and rocks, and we used small pruning shears to cut them apart and get them off rather than the time it would take to unwrap every knot.

After the rush of water from the pipe bursting, there were a lot more exposed roots along the sides of the creek, and parts of it had eroded away dramatically, leaving shorn sides that dropped off in places.

Usually, I would be more focused on the bigger pieces, but since we had so many other teams working, including Blakely's just across the way, we took our time and got every bit we could find. Bottle caps, cigarette butts, nails and other things had settled at the bottom of the water. This portion was clear for the most part and running smoothly. It wasn't deep, so we could easily reach most of the refuse we spotted.

I had the audacity to actually say aloud, "This is going really well," when we had reached the underside of the bridge.

Right then, someone from Blakely's team let out a disgusted shriek.

"Ew ew ew," he was yelling.

"What is it?" Sam called over. Our groups were really close together now, so leaving our garbage bags on the west creek bank, we stepped across to the other side using a few rocks to stay mostly out of the water.

"I don't know, but it's really freaking gross," Blakely, who was typically a pretty tough kid, looked pale as a ghost and like she might puke any second.

Byron and I exchanged glances, and I pulled my bandana around my nose.

"Let me see." I grimaced and walked over to the area they had all backed away from.

Sure enough, just like what Byron and I had seen the other day, there was a black shadow that looked and moved like Jell-O.

Using a stick, Byron poked at it like we had before, and it slithered down into the water, the smell going with it and, like before, leaving strands of greasy black hairs that dissolved into the water.

"What was that?" a girl I recognized from maybe my lunch hour asked, holding her nose with a grimace.

"I do not know," I said.

"Well, I'm done now, so." The girl and another boy gave a thumbs-up to Blakely, holding their noses with their other hands.

"I actually have to head out too." Sam grabbed two of the fullest bags. "Told my mom I'd walk Mo. But I'll take these to the truck."

"Thank you," Blakely said, and the two from her group who were leaving helped grab the bags that were ready from the other group. "Now that whatever that smell was is gone, I'm gonna keep going. We're pretty close."

I agreed, and Byron and I hopped back to the other side.

Lyla was looking on curiously, and I gave her an out. "You want to head home too?"

"What and miss possibly finding something else dead? No way." Lyla picked up the empty bag, and we began walking.

"I don't think it was dead." Meara was staring across the water at the place where the blob had been.

"Do you know what it was?" I asked, brow furrowed.

"I don't think it was dead," she repeated.

"You said that already." A look of concern flitted across Byron's face.

"If it isn't something dead, what is it?" I asked.

"Eroding," Meara whispered. "The water is deep enough."

"What did you just say?" I didn't think I could have heard right.

But she repeated, "The water is deep enough."

"That's what Frankie was saying." I gave Byron a quizzical look.

"Eroding," Meara said, still whispering. "We should leave."

"What's she talking about?" Lyla asked. Byron looked equally confused.

"I don't know." I grabbed my tools and the extra bags. "But I think we should listen to her."

The others nodded, and we turned to go.

Just then, a scream echoed across the park.

Chapter 18

My instinct was to run from the sound. But Byron and Lyla took off toward it, so I allowed myself time for a groan, then followed them.

When we got to the mouth of the creek channel we had been cleaning up, everyone paused to listen. The sound of screaming had been replaced by shouting and, listening closer, laughter.

"What the heck?" Blakely rolled her eyes, and the group walked toward the sound. The ruckus grew louder as we got closer.

A crowd of other students was on one of the low wooden bridges that crossed the water, and a girl from one of my classes was having it out with Jack, who was laughing the hardest.

"Y'all okay?" Byron asked as we walked up to the crowd of about a dozen students. Most of them were laughing, though a few seemed to be doing so nervously, except for the girl whose name I finally remembered.

"Emily, are you okay?" I asked.

"What happened?" Lyla asked someone in the group.

"I'll tell you what happened." Emily was fuming. I didn't know her very well, but I hadn't expected such fire to come from someone just barely over five feet, which was perhaps height-ist on my part. Was that a thing?

Anyway, she was livid.

"This absolute butt-hole hid under this bridge and grabbed my ankle while I was walking past." She was shaking and hot, angry tears spilled down her cheeks.

"Chill out," Jack said through chuckles. "It was just a prank."

"A creepy as heck prank, Jack. You know how much I hate being scared." She reached out like she was going to slap him.

But Byron stepped gently between them. "Come on," he said. "Let's get out of here."

She let him lead her, and a couple of sympathetic friends away.

"Not cool, Jack." I scowled. "You shouldn't be messing around like that."

He was dripping wet, and black mud and green algae streaked his shirt from where he'd climbed into the water.

"It was just a joke. Lighten up." He swiped his bangs out from his eyes, leaving traces of swamp water.

"Even if you didn't know how freaked out she was going to be, you still shouldn't be pranking our volunteers." I handed him a pair of gloves and an empty bag. "Get back to work and probably, like, I dunno, apologize to her. That was really mean."

As I walked away from Jack and the group, I heard him say to Blakely, "I mean, it was objectively funny, right?"

I was relieved when Blakely replied, "Shut up, dude."

Lyla, Byron, and I joined up with Emily's group for the rest of the cleanup. Emily was clearly shaken, but I didn't want to pry. She was the one who offered the information as we walked along the water, parallel to the path.

"My brother, Aedan, was one of the ones who almost drowned last time." She explained. "I know your sister and you, like, saved him."

"It was mostly luck." I picked another candy wrapper out of a bed of leaves.

"Well, I've obviously been jumpy since then. It was a big scare for all of us."

"Oh, I'm sure. I know what it's like to almost lose a sibling." I didn't elaborate, but she wrapped me in a hug. Which was surprising, since I barely knew her, and also adorable.

"I'm really glad you all were there." My shoulder muffled her voice as she gave me a squeeze.

"Me too."

"He's been acting kind of weird though," she added.

"How so?" I asked.

She shrugged, "It's probably nothing. Little brother stuff."

We parted and kept walking.

I glanced up and caught Lyla staring at us. But when I gave her an "I really don't know what just happened" shrug, she gave me a genuine smile and kept cleaning up.

I did not know what was going on between the two of us and made a mental note to have some best friend alone time with Byron as soon as possible. He was definitely going to be interested in how uninterested I was in the hug I got from Emily, who was maybe flirting but I really wasn't sure.

Our two groups continued cleaning up for about an hour, and we had made fantastic progress when there was another scream, this time from ahead of us.

"We better go see what it is now." I was getting pretty tired of all the extra volunteers and drama that was apparently accompanying the larger numbers. When we rounded the corner and saw that it was, yet again, Jack causing the issue, I considered the fact that we might not have a volunteer problem but a Jack problem.

"Cut it out, dude. Come on." Blakely was standing above him on a bridge that was similar to the one from before but a little higher.

Jack was flailing about in the water, looking like he was trying to climb up but then falling back.

"Can he swim?" Lyla asked as we all jogged over.

"It's not even deep over there." Byron pointed out. "You can just stand up."

"What is he doing?" I asked, puzzled.

"I don't know, and I really don't care," Emily said, and she and her group just kept right on walking back toward the cars.

"Come on, man. Just grab my hand." Blakely reached out to Jack, who looked like he was full-on panicking.

"Something just swam past my leg," he shouted, his face pale and frantic.

"That's a line from *Star Wars*, you nerd. Now climb out. I'm tired of this." Blakely looked almost embarrassed about her friend.

"Seriously, I can't get out," Jack was yelling now.

"This isn't worth our time anymore." Byron tapped Blakely on the shoulder, and everyone started walking away.

Then Jack started laughing. "Okay, okay, sorry."

He stood up and sure enough, the water was maybe three feet deep where he was. He waded toward the bridge and Blakely's outstretched hand to haul him onto the wood, but when he was about two yards away, he dropped under the water.

"Ugh, I can't believe him." Blakely stomped her foot.

But Jack was under for a beat. Then two.

I kept expecting him to pop up on the other side of the bridge and yell, "Boo."

But he was under for a breath. Then another.

"Um," Lyla said. "How good of a swimmer is he?"

"A really shitty one," Blakely said then yelled, "Jack, you better show us where you are, you jerk. I'm getting really ticked off."

But there was nothing. No splashing. No stifled giggles.

I realized I had been holding my breath, listening.

"Something's wrong," Byron said, moving quickly to the other side of the bridge and looking down to see if Jack had swum under.

"Jack!" Blakely shouted.

The water didn't move. There was no sound. I noticed that even the birds and wind had stopped. It was silent.

I didn't even realize I was about to jump into the water until Meara was suddenly beside me, her hand on my upper arm.

"Don't," she said.

In almost the same breath, Blakely jumped in, frantically walking toward the spot where Jack had gone under the water.

"We have to help." I took a step forward, and Meara's grip on my arm tightened.

Byron turned toward us and was kicking off his shoes to follow Blakely.

"No," Meara said firmly, putting her hand in the center of Byron's chest.

"What? Meara, stop," Byron said, moving her hand, but she replaced it.

"Don't."

The look in Meara's eyes was scared and deep.

Two other friends that had been in Blakely's group had followed her into the water, and they were all searching.

"Meara, why?" I asked.

She worked her jaw back and forth. I could almost hear her teeth grinding as she did.

"Erosion." She spoke through gritted teeth.

"Meara, I don't understand." I wanted to. But it was hard to concentrate over the sound of the students pushing through the water, shouting Jack's name.

"It's crowded in there." Lyla was suddenly beside me too. Or had she been there the whole time?

"He's gone," Meara said. "They won't find him."

"Meara, he just went in, like, a minute and a half ago. He's got to be there."

Meara shrugged.

"We need to go get the adults and call 911," I said.

"I'll go," Lyla took off toward the park entrance quickly, pulling her phone out of her pocket as she ran.

"I'll go with her," Byron said, and hurried up the path after her.

"Let's go," Meara said. "They're not going to find him."

"We can't just leave." I still couldn't stop scanning the water, which was now churned up from all the activity Jack and his friends were causing.

Meara shrugged and turned away, walking toward the back entrance to the neighborhood rather than the parking lot.

"Meara, wait." I caught up to her. "I don't think it's safe to go that way alone."

She smiled at me sadly. "Don't worry about me. I'll be fine."

I turned back to the chaos. Blakely came out of the water, shaking and looking distraught, her long hair slick with algae and dripping wet.

"Byron and Lyla are getting the teachers and calling 911." I didn't know what to say. I kept expecting Jack to pop out of the brush next to the water or from underneath the bridge.

But surely, we would have heard him by now. Even with all the shouting.

Blakely's head drooped, and her fists dug into the moss at the edge of the rock where she sat, still staring into the water. One by one, her friends stopped looking and went to sit dripping next to each other, out of breath and covered in grime.

For the second time in a month, Byron led first responders to the water. This time it was firefighters too. They carried long poles and had on wading pants and began dredging the creek. A news crew came as well, to cover the search for the missing teen, who had disappeared in front of a half dozen sets of eyes.

But we were able to leave before it showed up.

I gave a statement, along with Byron and Lyla. We all left out Meara though. There were so many kids to talk to, they didn't press any of us after we all said the same things.

When we were leaving, we passed a stricken Emily, who I guessed was having a way worse time of it than most of the rest of us. I gave her a quick hug, and we piled into my mom's van.

All the neighborhood had heard about it, and our parents were there to meet us and drive us home, even though it was barely any distance. Ma took the truck and offered to unload what trash bags we'd remembered to get out of the park. The rest I decided we could take care of tomorrow. The garbage wasn't going anywhere.

"Maybe we should volunteer at, like, the zoo or something next time?" Byron suggested.

"Do you think they'll find him?" Lyla asked.

But I shook my head. "I don't think so."

Kneeling in waist-deep water.

There are bags everywhere.

Plastic and full of contaminants. Unerodable. Uncompostable. Going nowhere.

Barriers for plant roots and suffocating the soft mosses. Tangling in the branches, water flowing the wrong way.

Its concern is what brought them here.

You feel the slick blackness.

You sense its confusion and bubbling anger.

They must stop. There must be a way to stop them.

Watching another one dragged against the decayed bank, you smell something familiar but continue your work.

Chapter 19

Before we'd even gotten home, my other mom texted me an appointment reminder for Dr. Duncan, which meant she'd scheduled one while we were on the way.

We dropped off Lyla and Byron then got home.

"I'll be down for dinner." I made my way up to the shower, though it was tempting to just stay grubby and eat something straight from the fridge right then. But my parents said we could order whatever I wanted to, and my grumbling stomach could wait for Vietnamese delivery.

My priority was to wash all the humid marsh air off. If people kept getting hurt or going missing at the park, it was going to lose the charm. I hated watching so many fond memories get rewritten by these accidents and tragedies.

Maybe they'd find him, I thought as I peeled off my work pants and shirt and tossed them into the hallway to take downstairs later.

I cranked the hot water up as high as I could stand, promising the environment that my next half dozen showers would be lukewarm to make up for it. I was too shaken up from the day to worry about whatever might be in the drain. It was like, as soon as I turned around, I could ignore what had happened behind me.

I dried off and went to my room, where Frankie sat up on her bunk, still in pajamas.

"Have you been up at all today?" I pulled a clean shirt out of the drawer and shuffled around for some comfortable shorts.

"What happened?" She cut right to the chase. "I heard there was...hubbub."

"It was Jack," I pulled on pants and, grabbing a brush, climbed up to sit with her on the worn galaxy comforter.

"What was Jack?" she asked, putting a bookmark in the novel she'd been looking at.

"He drowned, they think? Maybe? He's missing. I don't really know."

"Were you there?" Frankie asked, looking at me intently.

"Yeah, we all were." But I realized that wasn't totally true. "Well, me and Byron and Lyla."

Frankie nodded. "Where was Meara?"

"She left right after." It hadn't even occurred to me until that moment to reach out to her and Sam. I grabbed my phone from my dresser and shot them both "you okay?" texts.

Meara responded with a thumbs-up almost immediately. Sam didn't, but that was pretty typical Sam, especially since he was probably still walking Mojito and his parents had strict no-phones policies about family time.

"I think they're still looking for him," I said.

Frankie shrugged. "Could have been worse."

"What?" I couldn't have heard right. Frankie had some dark humor sometimes, but this seemed out of character.

"Just saying." She shrugged again and opened up her book. "Better Jack than you."

I let it go. I was tired, and even if I didn't want anyone else to drown, I definitely didn't want to drown either.

"Right, well, thanks I guess." I hopped off the top bunk and flopped onto my own. "Wake me up for dinner."

Then it was lights out. I slept harder than I thought I'd ever slept before and woke up to Ma knocking on our door to let us know dinner was ready. Afternoon light slanted through our windows, and I could tell it was at least a few hours since I'd laid down.

I rolled out of bed and, glancing at Frankie's bunk, registered that she was actually up for the first time in what seemed liked days. I followed my mom to the dining room, where my stomach made a happy yearning sound at the first whiff of Bun Chi Gou and imperial rolls, my favorite.

"Where's Frankie?" I asked, tucking in.

"Oh, she said she's having dinner with Meara." Mom passed me the fluffy white rice, and I heaped it onto my plate.

I was eating so quickly my folks had to remind me to chew, but I was famished after the long day.

"Do you have any plans with your friends tonight, or are you staying in?" Mom asked.

"The second one." I had a mouth full of egg roll when I answered.

"Well, if you want to have someone over, you could."

I stopped chewing and looked between my parents, who were clearly trying to be chill.

"Anyone in particular y'all have in mind?" I asked.

They looked at me with uncannily similar expressions. "Just thought your new friend might want to come over. Especially since today was so much." Ma said, giving Mom a knowing look.

136

"Oh my gosh, you two are ridiculous." I could tell they wanted details and were also trying not to pry at the same time.

"We would just like to meet her is all and thank her for the help when Frankie was sick. But if you want to just take it easy after your day, we understand that too. Just thought you might appreciate some company." Mom handed me another napkin as she said it.

"Yeah, I'm sure that's what you wanted to have her over for." I rolled my eyes, shoveling the last bite of spring roll into my mouth. "For the record, I might just invite her over. But not because you two suggested it." I pointed a finger back and forth between the two of them.

Mom chuckled, and Ma said, "Just remember to keep your door cracked open."

"Listen, I'm about half a second from going full-blown nineties teenager and stomping out of here in a huff." I stood and took my plate to the sink.

"We can't help it if we're such a textbook family unit."

On my way back to my room, I flipped open my phone and called Lyla, who picked up on the second ring.

"Hey." Her voice was groggy and muffled.

"Oh, no, did I wake you up?"

"Yeah, but that's okay. What time is it?"

"Like, half past seven." I felt bad. "I'm sorry I woke you up."

"Really, don't worry about it, I shouldn't sleep all day. Otherwise, I'll be up at, like, two." I heard the sound of sheets rustling and Lyla taking a drink of water. "Anyway, what's up?"

"I was just wondering if you wanted to come over and keep me company? You know, busy day and all?"

It felt like an hour before she answered, but it was probably two seconds on the outside.

"Sounds good. I'll be there in twenty." Then she hung up.

"Oh, that was easy," I said to myself.

"So, she's coming over?" a voice down the hallway said, and I about jumped out of my skin until I saw both my moms peeking around the corner.

"Don't sneak up on me like that!" I said.

But they didn't care and just chuckled.

Lyla arrived exactly fifteen minutes later, and I gave my parents a full five minutes of introduction time while I waited for popcorn to finish popping.

"Okay, you met," I said. "Now we're going to watch a movie."

"Enjoy movie time," Mom said.

Ma followed up with, "We'll poke our heads in, just in case you need anything."

Which was an absolutely not subtle way of making sure that we knew they could interrupt us at any moment.

"So, what are we watching?" Lyla asked, plopping down on the soft rug and leaning against the bottom bunk like she had when she'd come over the other day. Lucifer came right up and demanded Lyla relinquish pets, to which she promptly complied.

I liked how comfortable she seemed in my space. It was a bonus that Luce liked her too. Or at least accepted the pets.

"I'm trying to decide if I want to suggest something intellectual to impress you." I sat down next to her and pulled over a small coffee table we had for this purpose to set the laptop onto.

"You're trying to impress me, huh?"

"Well…" I paused, pulling up the browser and streaming service. "I'm at least trying to not scare you off."

"I don't think that's possible." Lyla laughed and pulled a throw blanket across her lap. "But I take it as a challenge, so please, try to scare me off."

I hadn't meant to let her know that I knew every single line to the 1995 classic *Empire Records*, but an hour and a half later, that's where we were.

"I can't believe you've never seen that movie," I said when it was done.

"I can't believe—no, wait." She paused. "I actually can totally believe that you have seen that movie seven hundred times."

"Want to watch it again?" I teased.

"You actually would, wouldn't you?" She laughed and clicked play again.

"Wait, no, I was joking." But when I reached over to pause it, she batted my hand away playfully.

"We're watching with the captions on this time, so I can follow along. It's very distracting with you reciting the entire thing next to me."

"This is silly," I said as the music started up. "I'm getting more snacks."

"Okay, I'll be here studying what makes Jean tick." Lyla mimed taking notes on a pad.

I was grinning so hard my cheeks were in danger of cracking while I popped more popcorn and grabbed some trail mix and LaCroix. I practically skipped back to my room. I couldn't remember the last time I'd had so much fun, and that she was even entertaining the idea of watching my favorite movie again was making my stomach do very acrobatic things.

Using my hip to open the door, my hands full of snacks, I stopped short then hurried in and closed the door behind me.

Lyla was standing now, her body cast a glow in the light of the still playing movie.

On the other side of the room, standing side by side just inside the now open window, stood Frankie and Meara.

Both dripping wet, puddles forming on the wooden floor beneath their bare and muddy feet.

"We found Jack," Frankie let out.

"Sam's with him," Meara breathed.

Chapter 20

"What are you doing?" I hissed. Lucifer had jumped off Lyla's lap and was weaving her way between Frankie's legs. "Is Jack okay?"

"The water is deep enough." Meara's words were slurred and unsteady. She made a movement with her chin and throat that made it look like she was about to vomit.

"You have to come with us." Frankie was suddenly a flurry of jerky movement, rushing to our closet and wrenching it open. Then pulling out camping gear that I didn't even remember we had. In seconds, she was tossing both me and Lyla climbing pants and thermal shirts.

I watched in horror as she tossed the blue hamster sweater I hadn't seen since middle school at my date.

Wait, was Lyla my date?

Despite the fact that Frankie was mid-seventies-rock-band level destruction of our room, I was worried that Lyla might realize I was a dork.

Probably too late for that.

"Get changed." Frankie continued to rummage around, pulling things from the closet.

I looked between her and Lyla, who was eyeing Meara with concern.

"Are you okay?" Lyla stepped toward Meara, who held up a hand and made another gagging sound. Lyla took another step closer, and Meara let out a groan.

"No." Meara backed away.

The noises coming from her throat sounded like she was choking or trying to throw up. She hit the frame of the open window and turned around, her head out into the open air as something came up from her gut.

Lyla and I both started toward her, but Frankie stepped between us.

"She'll be okay in a second." Frankie handed both of us camping hats. "Put these on."

"Frankie, what is happening?" I demanded as Lyla put her hat on.

"I..." Frankie began then clamped her mouth shut and let out a shudder. She closed her eyes and took a deep breath. Like the ones I took when I was trying to regain control of my body and regulate my system to prevent a panic attack.

She shook her head and then looked at me, her eyes sharp and fierce. "Trust me."

Frankie was always so laid back. The chill sister who was up for anything. She'd never asked anything of me.

I gave her a short nod. "Yes."

Meara was still coughing, and Lyla and I kept our distance. A few moments later, Meara stopped and turned around, her skin chalky and streaks of mud smeared across her mouth, where she tried to wipe it off with her sleeve.

Frankie tossed her a towel from the laundry pile, and Meara wiped the rest of the muck off.

"Try not to touch it," Frankie said. I took Lyla's hand, and the two of us stepped back a bit more.

Both Meara and Frankie could obviously hear us, but we whispered anyway.

"Do you have any idea what is going on?" Lyla was looking at the other two, worry written all over her face.

"No, but I have to trust my sister." I truly did not know what was happening, but if Frankie was involved, I would be too. "I have to keep her safe if I can."

Lyla turned back toward me and squeezed the hand she was still holding. "But what about keeping you safe?"

"We have to go. We don't have much more time." Frankie said as she and Meara made for the door.

"Hang on. I have to meet you out front," Lyla said. "I don't think your parents will be very happy if I overstay my welcome."

"Good point. I'll walk you out."

Frankie and Meara exchanged looks that I could not interpret.

"Okay." Meara climbed through the open window, and Frankie slipped out behind her while Lyla and I walked downstairs. At the last second, I pulled off the beanie that Frankie had tossed my way, realizing my folks would think it was quite odd for me to be wearing one, given my plans to just go to bed.

"It was really nice to meet you," Mom said.

Lyla grinned, waving goodbye. "You too."

"Come back anytime." Ma and I waved at Lyla. I shut the door before they could say anything else.

"Right, I'm going to bed," I said, yawning an actual real yawn, and hurried without seeming like I was hurrying to my room.

"Have a good night's rest," my mom called, and I gave a thumbs-up without looking back.

When I got back to our room, I considered just closing and locking the windows, but that wouldn't keep Frankie out for long. I quickly pulled on the rest of the clothes that Frankie had put out for me and locked the bedroom door before climbing out the window. Scaling the bricks like usual, I dropped down onto the grass and scurried across the yard where the others were crouched.

But it was only Meara and Frankie.

"Where's Lyla?" I whispered, looking around the yard where I expected her to be coming from, though she should have beat me by a full three minutes.

In the darkness, I could see Meara shrug.

"She's still out front." Frankie nodded to the gate.

"I need to go talk to her."

"We can't wait long." Frankie stayed crouched.

"Hey, wait just, like, one minute, maybe two. I'll be quick."

But Frankie spun around. "We cannot wait any longer than that." She hissed. "Hurry, or we'll have to go without you."

I hurried that way and found her on the curb.

"My folks just called. I have to go." She frowned, her eyebrows furrowed in concern. "You sure following them is a good idea?"

"I don't really have a choice." It was the second time in just a few days that Frankie had dragged me into the darkness of the night. "She has to have a good reason for it. I know you don't know Frankie, but I do. If she knows where Jack is and says Sam is there too, then I have to believe her and go."

"Just be careful and please let me know when you make it home." She gave me a quick hug, and I was too scared of what I might be walking into to be scared of hugging her back.

She smelled really nice.

I gave her a last squeeze and rushed after Frankie and Meara.

We walked in silence to the edge of the park, the quiet eerie and unusual. It would have been hard for me to keep up with Meara and Frankie. But every twenty yards or so, Meara had to stop and catch her breath, and every once in a while, Frankie stumbled.

Meara seemed to be choking back a cough. Trying to keep things quiet. Each time, my instinct was to go up and whack her on the back to help, but Frankie held me off.

"What's wrong with her?" I whispered, knowing my concern must be showing on my face, even in the partial moonlight.

Frankie just shook her head.

"You can tell me, whatever it is." I was imagining any number of things. Maybe drugs. Maybe an allergy. Maybe mixing up meds. Meara and Frankie had been acting strange for days now, and I wanted to know what was going on.

Frankie didn't say anything for a moment, just stared back at me, searching my face and not finding whatever she was looking for.

Meara let out a small noise then hissed. "Okay, I'm fine. Let's go."

"That is obviously a lie." I crossed my arms.

"We don't have time for this." Meara turned away from us and continued on.

"Jean." Frankie was still peering at me intently. "Please."

"Fine." I followed her as she caught up with Meara. In my head, I was making a list of all the ways I would be pulling this out as a sibling trump card in the future.

When we got about fifty feet from the park entrance, Meara cut to the right and stepped through the trees.

There had been rain the past few days off and on, so we were able to move through the wooded part in near silence, though it slowed us down. Meara and Frankie were taking their time, hunched low. They seemed to meld into the underbrush, floating across the mulch and wet leaves and small branches. I felt like a plodding oaf, aware of every shaky sound I was making.

Finally, they stopped, and Frankie held her finger to her lips. I could make out her glassy eyes in the darkness.

"We're close," she breathed then pointed across the water.

At first, I couldn't tell what I was looking at because it was too big to process.

Then the shape came into focus.

A dark green shadow waded in the deepest part of the swampy area. It moved slowly, its arms swinging as it lumbered across the marsh.

"Slowly," Frankie breathed, and she inched forward to a low spot where we were on the bank. Tied to a branch was a flatboat, and she stepped into it and laid down, the water barely rocking as she did so.

My whole body protested. I didn't want to get anywhere near that water.

But she looked at me. "We have to get closer."

I shook my head but stepped gingerly into the raft, holding onto the sides to steady myself. Meara climbed down, but she did not get in. Instead, she crouched and gave the boat a push.

Within one bend of the creek, we could hear them.

Chapter 21

"You. Have to." Frankie barely made a sound, and I looked at her, panic clearly written all over my face.

Her eyes were closed, and she was grinding her teeth so hard I could hear them scraping against one another and her jaw popped.

I shook my head at her with a small movement. I didn't want to rock the paddle boat we were laying flat in. I took a breath and almost jumped out of my skin when I felt her grab my hand and put something small into it with barely a movement.

Resisting the urge to ask her what it was, I quickly pulled it to my face, and in the dim moonlight, I could make out the distinctive shape of one of my emergency panic attack pills.

My mind and my body were not happy about anything that was happening. But I popped it into my mouth, swallowing the tiny, white pill dry for not the first time.

Frankie knew as well as I did that the meds would work fast, especially with how hard my blood was pumping. I didn't want to think about what I should do next, but when I looked at Frankie, she just nodded and tilted her head toward the bodies we had seen before ducking out of sight.

"It's not here." Frankie spoke in a way that made it seem she was having to manually push the air past her vocal cords.

I squeezed my eyes shut. "Are you sure?"

She shook her head, tears leaking from the corners of her eyes.

Another moan pierced the night air. I didn't know who was making the noise, but that shouldn't matter. I shouldn't be here. We should be calling our parents or, like whoever, the Oklahoma version of Mulder and Scully is.

Frankie took my hand again. "Fast." Then she shook her head in that jerky way. "Slow. Like. Quicksand."

We were seriously going to have words with one another when we got back to bed. But more than anything, I wanted to *get* back to bed, and I knew Frankie—she wouldn't be asking me to do something like this as a joke.

And I'd seen the bodies around the next curve of the creek before we'd paddled back out of sight.

Taking a breath, I kicked off my shoes, leaving them at the bottom of the small boat. Before I could overthink it more, or the panic meds wore off, I took a breath and turned over so I was kneeling on all fours then stepped over the side and slid into the marshy water.

I ignored the images of gar and alligator snapping turtles and those super creepy fish with human teeth that flashed through my brain and half swam, half waded toward the alcove we had passed, trying my best to make no noise as I worked my way across the swampy pond. Though it was only two dozen yards away, I snagged my leggings more than once, having to keep from yelping as I removed spiky branches from my path.

Rounding the corner, even in the darkness, I could see three bodies, each one embedded into the roots of the tree stretching down the bank. The branches and vines had been raked through and made to wrap around the figures. Each was partially coated in the same black slime we'd been encountering, and I had to remind myself to breathe to keep from passing out, trying to avoid the smell.

If I hadn't heard their cries, I would have assumed all three figures were dead, but they were each vocalizing. Pain at the best, despair at the worst. It reminded me of the "bring out your dead" scene in *Monty Python and the Holy Grail*, and I had to stifle hysterical laughter threatening to bubble out of me. And that movie was going to be forever ruined because of this moment.

But then I recognized Sam's mop of hair, and the urge to protect him swelled in me, propelling me toward the figure on the far left.

"Sam," I whispered as I neared him, wincing at the sound of squelching mud as I made my way up the small bank.

He looked at me briefly, then his eyes rolled back in his head, and if he hadn't been attached to the wall, I guessed he would have passed out flat on his back like a mannequin pushed over by an angry Black Friday shopper who missed a deal.

Doing my best not to make noise, I pulled myself toward him with about as much grace as a flamingo trying to push a shopping cart.

Using the branches as leverage, I half climbed, half waded until we were eye level. I tugged at the branches that were holding him to the bank. They came loose more easily than I had expected. I considered daring a sigh of relief, but then I heard a noise I did not recognize.

A suctioning slurp of something large pulling its way toward the bodies and me.

Frankie had said that it was gone.

It might have been.

But it was clearly back.

My brain was really going to have some fight-or-flight unpacking to do with my therapist.

Fleeing was not an option. I couldn't leave Sam to whatever plan that thing had. Last I checked, boogie men didn't strap kids to creek walls to give them scholarships or summer job offers.

The sound grew closer.

Barely breathing, I pulled myself under the last few branches that were holding Sam and wedging myself next to him as best I could, maneuvered behind him, wrapping my arms around his waist, and pulled us both back against the wall.

I strained against his weight, threatening to topple forward since I'd already pulled out most of the branches propping him up.

The weight of the air shifted as it got closer. The mud itself seemed to swell against us, pushing me forward as I clawed into Sam's sweatshirt, trying not to make a sound.

Arms trembling, I made myself remember to breathe. To not lock my knees.

Five things I see. The back of Sam's neck. Brown branches from the tree above me. The reflection of the moon on the water. A tree. The collar of Sam's sweatshirt.

Four things I smell. Jack's Axe body spray. Even from here. Popcorn on my breath. The dirt behind me. The rank scent that was becoming familiar. The black goo now right under my grip.

Three things I feel. My grip on Sam, probably leaving nail marks on his chest. The ground throbbing now, undulating like an earthquake, but only here, in this mud. The reverberating shatter of bone.

Two things I hear. The reverberating shatter of bone. Tearing of tissue from skeleton.

One thing I taste. Blood.

I've bitten my tongue.

Even with the meds and the exercise, I was still on the verge of a panic attack. Because this was too much.

But my mind was blank, and I couldn't think of a single other breathing exercise. So, I started over.

Five things I see.

But my eyes were closed so tight I was going to get a headache. Probably going to stay that way forever if I had to guess. If I survived this, I supposed it would be without a sense of humor. Or else a drastically more morbid one.

Staying grounded was exactly what I didn't want to do.

But that was when I heard a sound that wasn't one I would give my left arm to forget.

It was banging. Of wood on metal. And shouts.

Someone was using our gazebo to make a distraction. Or something else loud.

The thing stopped its own horrible sounds, and the silence was so deafening for a few moments that I thought maybe I imagined the banging. But then I heard it again, and so did the monster that was munching on its dinner. At the sound of the second set of loud bangs and shouts, the creature dropped something heavy into the water and turned toward the noise.

I kept breathing shallowly for ten more breaths as the thing, whatever it was, continued moving away.

I was going to kill Frankie if we all made it out of this alive.

Walking purposefully to collect another, there is a pounding sound.
You pause and listen.
It is out of place, and you cannot understand its origin.
Moving on leaden legs, you change directions slowly and move toward the banging sound.
It should be quieter here. There should be fewer noises. The nighttime is already full of noises.
You turn toward the sound. You would like to make it stop.

Chapter 22

I let myself take a breath as soon as the sound of the creature was at least more distant than before. I could hear it sloshing through the boggy waters.

Not losing any time, I pushed my way around to Sam's front again and wrenched the branches out of the way.

Instead of being solely focused on stealth, I decided it was time to balance that with speed and nope the heck out of there.

With an oomph, I got Sam away from the wall, the weight of his body slumped against me, but when I lowered him down, he floated in the water enough that I could drag him away.

Don't look back. Is what I should have done.

But I looked back.

The furthest of the remaining two figures was decimated. There was almost nothing left. I doubted there would be anything left by morning.

The second, I realized when I finally got up the courage to really look closely, was Jack.

And he was looking at me, eyes wide, body unmoving.

"Please," he whispered through clenched, unmoving jaws. "Jean."

I couldn't take them both at once. There was no way.

"I'll be back," I said as softly as I could, moving toward the bend in the water around the corner of which I really hoped Frankie had at least left the boat. The banging in the distance was still loud. I needed Sam to run. There was no way the creature was moving so slowly that it wouldn't catch up to them soon.

Which meant it would either catch them or not.

And be back here soon.

"Fuck," I said, doubling my speed and dragging Sam, still totally covered in muck—but less of the rancid black type—to the small boat and, with some surprise reserve of energy, rolled him into it.

As I did, he moaned, and I paused for a moment to make sure he wasn't going to wake up and start screaming.

Frankie was nowhere to be seen, and I was so full of adrenaline I didn't stop to think about where she might have wandered off to.

I had often questioned why heroes in horror movies sometimes wound up wearing so few items of clothing, but as I discarded my sweatshirt and lamented my long tangle of hair, I understood why.

I needed to hurry.

Instead of keeping to the water and wading slowly this time, I scrambled on the edge of the bank using the branches to keep my balance, making faster—though not quieter—progress, pausing every few minutes to make sure I could hear the sound of the creature moving away and not closer.

I reached Jack much more quickly than I had reached Sam, but he was somehow in worse shape. Purple bruises raked across his face, and he appeared to be totally unconscious when I got to him.

"Jack," I hissed quietly, shaking him gently on the shoulder. He moaned and then jerked his head up with a start.

I clamped my hand over his mouth and whispered quickly, "It's me. Stay quiet."

He nodded slightly, and I pulled my hand away, wrapping it around the vines that held him in place and prying them from around him as well as I could.

Jack kept nodding off like Sam had, and I was not up for dragging his six-foot-four basketball-player self around a swamp in the middle of the night or ever. Maybe I should make it my next goal to get super swole and be able to firefighter carry someone three times my weight. But now was not the time to draw out a reward chart in my planner.

Jack was finally loose enough to slide out of the cage, and we both dropped into the water. It was easier to help him with the buoyancy it provided.

Then we heard it.

The thing.

Whatever it was stopped making noise. Which meant it had either found or decided to ignore the distraction the metal banging was providing.

I listened, moving us slowly toward the waiting boat, and then the sound changed as the thing turned back toward our direction.

It was in a hurry.

Not daring to even whisper, I dragged Jack with me, cringing every time the water made a splash. Every ten steps, I paused and listened, the slosh of the creature coming closer.

Jack was struggling to keep up, and then he stumbled on something. Could have been anything. The water here was only

chest deep and full of debris and sticks and rocks. And—
shudder—turtles.

Catching him before his head went under, I flipped him
onto his back like I knew what I was doing and grabbed him
under his arms, making sure his head rested on my shoulder.

Moving backward, I kept us as low and steady in the water
as I could.

Why the heck did he still smell like too much Axe body
spray? He'd been in a bog since who-knew-when. How was that
smell still lingering?

It was mid that super helpful thought that the swamp
monster must have reached the place it had been keeping its
snacks or whatnot and the sloshing and splashing and rustling
turned to an angry vibration.

"We have to move, Jack," I hissed, even though I was fairly
certain he was totally passed out. I pulled him along with me as
quickly as I could. We were almost to the boat with Sam.

The thing was starting to make more noise.

It sounded like it was hitting the water in a tantrum, making
the usually almost stagnant alcove where the boat was seem like
it was in choppy wakes.

Whatever it was, it was big enough to make waves upstream
in our little creek.

We reached the spot where I had rolled Sam into the boat,
and using some sort of reserve adrenaline, I pushed Jack up next
to him.

I let my head rest for a few moments on the edge of the
boat while I tried to think about what to do next.

Now what? I would have whispered to myself if I wasn't so
completely scared of making an unnecessary noise.

I listened. The monster didn't seem to get closer. Maybe Jack's body spray was masking its sense of smell. That would actually make sense. I was never going to smell Axe body spray without flashing back to this.

There was a rustling sound in the bushes, and I almost screamed but held it together for a few moments and peered into the shrubs.

The wagging tail was the dead giveaway.

"Scram," I whisper-yelled at Sam's dog. What the heck was she doing here? "Get on home."

But the stupid, adorable dog just stood there quietly, wagging her tail and looking like she was ready to hop into the creek for a swim.

"Mojito, go away," I hissed.

But she just did a playful crouch and dropped a stick near me like I was going to play fetch. When she realized I wasn't going to do that, she leapt into the water with a splash and jumped onto the boat, giving Sam a big lick across the cheek. Then, her tail wagging a mile a minute, she hopped back out and trotted into the woods.

I was torn in two—wanting to follow her until I could find a makeshift leash to lead her away from the park or actually focusing on saving my friends.

Well, friend and Jack.

I took a breath, and since I didn't have a piece of paper to write out all the tasks I needed to get done, nor did I have time to color code those tasks by urgency, I instead jumped right to the end.

"Get the boys. Out of the park." I looked behind me.

Where we had tucked the boat spilled out onto the main part of the water, and I would need to expose us to the big bad while we turned the corner. This cove wasn't going to hide us for long.

"To the right." I swam-slash-walked over to the other side of the boat and pushed it ahead of me. Without it, I would have needed to drag the boys separately, and that would have taken all night.

I could still hear the creature making angry sounds and splashing, but it was helpful for covering the small sounds we were making as I pushed the boat out into the open water.

The new goal was to get the boat to the small bridge on the far side of Stonefish Creek that led into the neighborhood. If the goal was "out of the park," it didn't do us much good if "out of the park" was super far from home.

Things went smoothly long enough for me to have the thought, *Things are going smoothly,* when suddenly the boat jerked to a stop with a much louder sound than I was expecting it to make.

I froze because, as soon as we made that noise, the sounds from behind us that the monster was making ceased.

We had its attention.

I did not want its attention.

As quietly as I could, I pushed on the boat to see if I could make it move. But it was stuck fast. Ducking low in the water, I walked to the other side of the boat and tried pulling, but it was stuck as well. Taking in a deep breath, I lowered myself and felt around until I found a log snagged on the bottom.

Prepping myself to not breathe out too loudly when I broke the surface, I took in a breath and dove down again. It wasn't deep at this part of the creek, and that made it easier to push while walking—and much harder now that the boat was wedged on top of a log.

"Why are you both so gigantic?" I muttered.

Looking toward the end of the creek, I considered taking them one at a time. But my arms were shaking, and I was losing focus.

Then I had an idea and began rocking the boat back and forth. Slowly, it moved a bit, but slowly wasn't really going to work for us. I rocked it again, jumping up on one end and putting my weight down on the edge to try to move it more quickly.

It was working, but we didn't have time.

The creature was large and loud and making its way toward us. For the—if I'm honest—eight hundredth time in the past ten minutes, I considered leaving the boys to it.

I jumped again, and the boat moved toward me a bit more. But I wasn't sure I could free it in time to put any distance between us and the monster. Then I heard a sound that made the bottom of my stomach drop out.

Mojito was barking like she wanted someone to throw her ball for her again.

Barking at the thing.

Leading it away from us.

"No no no no." I jumped again and used as much of my weight as I could to tip the boat toward me.

After two more tries, it broke free with a splash.

Moving as quickly as I could, I rounded the boat and heaved it forward, making time even faster than I had before.

Not thinking about the Mojito situation because it might literally break me, I forced myself to move as fast as I could, and in minutes that felt like hours, we were under the small bridge and scraping the bottom of the boat on the cement of the neighborhood culvert.

"Almost home." I patted Sam, still fast asleep, on the shoulder, and collapsed heavily against the retaining wall.

Chapter 23

While I crouched in the brush on the far western side of the waterways, I was planning on having a full-blown, honest-to-goodness melt down, complete with post-comedown demands of mint chocolate chip ice cream from Braum's. I'd gotten the little boat—which was bogged down by the weight of Jack and Sam and their totally soggy clothes—as far as I could up the creek and into the cement drainage leading into our neighborhood.

But the water there was not deep enough to let me pull the boat any farther, and both Jack and Sam were passed out. Completely unresponsive, for the time being at least.

As quietly as I could, every few minutes, I'd shaken them both to make sure they were still capable of waking up. And without fail, every single time, they'd moaned, and I'd regretted trying to wake them up because whatever the heck that thing was still out there, even if it didn't seem to be following us for now.

I sat against a rock on the side of the culvert and took a breath for a few seconds while I figured out what to do.

"Hey," Frankie whispered, and it made me jump out of my skin, which in hindsight was not the best phrase to use.

But I stifled any shriek I might have shrieked and pointed toward the small boat.

"Where the heck were you?" I asked.

And immediately regretted my harsh tone since it finally occurred to me that it was probably Frankie drawing the monster thing's attention away from the rest of us.

"They alive?" she asked, putting her toe against Sam's leg and giving it a nudge. He stirred and she crouched down beside him gently cupping his face with her hand.

"Far as I can tell." I stood and tried pulling the boat along as I had been. But the weight of the two boys and the shallow and rockiness of the water made it impossible, and it was only adrenaline that made me wonder if I could keep going.

"They should go home." Frankie stood and wiped her hand on her jeans.

"Ya think?"

"Try to get them up." She stuck her hands in her jean jacket pockets and backed away a few paces. Her combat boots splashed in the water, and she went to stand by the embankment, leaning against the concrete siding.

"What, so you're just gonna freaking watch?" I hissed. Every sound we made felt like a bell ringing in a tower.

She didn't respond as I knelt by the boys and began waking them up. I realized I would probably have to do it one at a time and went with Sam first.

"Sam, hey, wake up. We gotta go, now." I pulled him to a seated position.

He managed to push himself to his feet. "Jean, where are we?"

I was grateful he asked quietly, practically whispering the question, but him wondering where we were after the literally countless hours we'd spent traipsing around these waterways together made me compartmentalize and assume it was a concussion or the lack of sunlight causing his confusion.

"We gotta get you home, like, as soon as possible." I stepped to his side and looped his arm around my shoulder.

"Oh crap, what happened to…" He turned and squinted at the second prone body. "Is that Jack?"

I nodded against his shoulder. "Come on. Let's get you home so I can help him next."

Sam stumbled a few times on wobbly legs, but we got to the top of the embankment, where what felt like wilderness turned into backyards.

We found our way through the familiar break between houses. There were a few homes we had known to avoid since we'd been young, and we knew which houses didn't care if we cut through their unfenced backyards.

Sam's house was close, and we got through the row of homes across from his when there was a shift in the air.

I grabbed the back of his completely disgusting and probably totally ruined shirt and yanked him down into a crouch in the shadow of some trashcans. The only light coming from a streetlamp two houses down.

I didn't have to shush Sam, but I did put my hand around him as he trembled and looked at me, eyes wide and questioning.

Giving him a squeeze, I closed my eyes and listened.

The neighborhood was silent. Like the park had been. No din of television drifting through the windows or cars driving past. No dogs barking. No birds or breeze or leaves.

When the motion sensor light on the side of the house where we were sitting as still as statues went on, I bit my lip to keep from screaming, and Sam squeezed my hand so hard I was sure I would cry out. But I didn't.

Whatever had triggered the light had to be close to us. I held my breath, waiting for it to come into view. But nothing did. I fought the urge to squeeze my eyes shut as hard as Sam was squeezing my hand, but I kept them trained on the sliver of yard I could see from where we hid. I counted to twenty in my head.

The light turned off.

Sam moved, but I pulled him down and shook my head slowly when he raised a panicked eyebrow at me.

Whatever had activated the light could have been waiting for us, as still as we were. I counted to twenty again tapping the seconds out with my finger on Sam's wrist, but the light didn't turn back on. Maybe it was just a cat or a branch or a blowing flag.

I gave Sam's hand a quick squeeze and stood up slightly, peering around the big recycling can. Looking around, I decided we shouldn't risk turning on the light ourselves, though most houses around here had them installed, primarily for opossums and raccoons. Pulling Sam up as well, I crawled-slash-ran across the small space between houses and crouched down behind the neighbor's trash receptacles, pushing Sam between the two ahead of me.

The air was heavy. Sticky humidity matted my already wet hair to my forehead, and if I stopped to daydream about jumping into a cool swimming pool at the start of June, I would never quit.

Still, the light did not turn back on, but the silence remained the same.

Until a dragging sound sliced through the air. Something pulling through the gravel. Or across concrete. Like chalk on a sidewalk. Brittle and rough.

Then with sudden brightness, the flood light came back on, and standing in the middle of the driveway, tail wagging and holding a freaking whole tree in her mouth, was Mojito.

I about collapsed with relief that the stupid dog was alive and that the dragging sound was the long-ass branch she held in her mouth.

Tail wagging, she dropped the stick and gave a little jump.

"She wants you to throw it," Sam said.

I burst into tears. "Can we just get you both home?"

Mo ran up to me and gave my face a big lick.

"Yeah, let's go," Sam said.

I got Sam through his front door.

"What are you going to tell your parents?" I asked.

He shrugged. "Anything I say is going to sound like a lie."

"I'm going to get Jack. See you tomorrow." I turned to leave, and Mojito whined and looked between me and Sam.

"I think she wants to go with you." Sam grabbed a leash off the hook by the door and handed it to me. "You can take her if you want and just bring her into the backyard when you're home."

I hesitated. I didn't want Mo running off at the monster again, but also her company sounded beyond nice. Clipping on the leash, I gave Sam a quick hug, and the two of us set off back the way we'd come for Jack.

When we got to him, he was awake with his head between his legs. Frankie stood a few feet away, arms crossed.

"Did I get wasted again?" he asked. I could see he'd gotten sick a ways away from where he now sat.

"I wish." It would have been much easier to explain to everyone if he'd just been drunk.

Mojito went over and gave him a nudge. He scratched behind her ears.

"Come on, Jack," I said. "I gotta get you home. Can you stand?"

He nodded. "Yeah, I think so. What happened?"

"You don't remember anything?" I asked. He shook his head. "That might be for the best. Come on, dude. There are a ton of people looking for you."

We got Jack to his front yard, his legs still unsteady, but I didn't want to be around when everyone found out he was alive and no longer missing. I wanted to be in my bed.

"You got it from here?" I asked, nodding at his front porch.

He said yeah, taking shaky steps up to the door.

"Do me a favor and just leave me out of whatever you tell the cops and your parents."

Before he stepped through it, he turned and said, "Thanks for something, Jean."

I chuckled, the adrenaline starting to leave my body.

"Sure, Jack." And I took Mojito with me into the dark street before the lights came on inside his house.

Giving Mojito a final hug, and making sure her back gate was closed, I got home before my legs gave way.

Chapter 24

"We have to tell our parents." I was practically vibrating as we climbed in through the window and collapsed on the floor, Frankie rolling away from me and coughing into her sleeve.

"No," she croaked.

"But why?" I didn't understand what was going on, but I knew with certainty that we were not going to be able to solve it on our own.

Frankie was in trouble. I would do anything to help her.

"Can't."

I threw my hands over my head and kicked off my muddy shoes, shoving them into a corner with my feet.

Reaching over to where my phone charged, I flipped it open to a text from Lyla. She asked me to text her when I got home and told me she was down an *Empire Records* soundtrack rabbit hole.

Watching that movie had been a lifetime ago.

"Right, you can't. I just have to trust you, even though there is obviously something very wrong." Turning my head toward her, I could see her jaw clenching, but she stared up at the ceiling, not looking at me. "You're really scaring me, Frankie."

She nodded slightly then whispered. "The water is deep enough."

When she turned to look at me, her face was slack, but there was a look in her eyes like she really wanted me to understand something I was just not getting.

"If this is freaking drugs, I'm going to be such a pain in the ass to live with." I pushed myself up to a seated position and assessed the absolute grime I was covered in. "I'm going to take a shower."

I knew it wasn't drugs. It couldn't be unless I was being drugged too. It just didn't make sense. I knew I was hearing and seeing things, but they would not add up in my brain to anything coherent.

"I think it killed a kid, Frankie. I think that's what I saw. We were too late." My voice quivered. I didn't hate the idea of a good long cry, but I wanted to shower first.

Frankie shook her head. "It was a deer."

"That's even worse!" I threw my hands up, and she tilted her head at me. "Okay, it's not worse. But Bambie?"

"We eat deer meat every year." Frankie pointed out, and she wasn't wrong.

But I shook my head. "Don't try to animal-murder logic me."

"It might not have been what killed it anyway." Frankie pulled off her boots.

"Oh really? Then how did a dead deer end up hooked to the side of the creek?"

"I dunno. But maybe it was hit by a car or something. I dunno."

"I feel like no one else but me is even trying to put two and two together."

I groaned and stood up, fully intending to stomp off. But the adrenaline had finally worn itself out of my system, and I wobbled. Bracing against the dresser, I took a breath. Usually, I would wait for my unsteadiness to pass before I'd take a shower. I had some fairly regular intrusive thoughts about slipping and smashing my head on tile, but there was no way I could sleep in the state I was in unless I was either willing to burn my dirty sheets afterward or sleep wrapped in a poncho.

"Will you please go with me?" I asked Frankie.

She nodded, and the two of us walked as quietly as we could to the bathroom.

I held Frankie's hand while the water from the showerhead beat down on me. I couldn't stand but managed to peel off my clothes and watched as the mud and grit from the water washed toward the spinning drain. I kicked the soggy pile to the side then pushed it out of the tub where I heard it splat on the floor.

Frankie didn't make a sound other than the occasional, "You okay, Jean?"

To which I had little or no response.

I let go of Frankie's hand long enough to lather my hair with shampoo and did my best to scrub the grime out from between my toes.

"I'm not really a mani-pedi person, but I think you're gonna owe me one." I stopped my hands from shaking by grabbing the conditioner and squeezing out about five times the amount I needed.

Frankie grunted in acknowledgment from the other side of the shower curtain.

Once, her hand began to slip away, and I couldn't help but grab it. "Stay. Please."

In response, she gave it a squeeze, and I let go to finish washing. By the time I was done, I was bone tired but able to stand on shaky legs. I turned off the faucet, watching the last of the sudsy water swirl down into the drain.

"Your turn." I wrapped a giant towel around myself and nodded toward the shower. "There should still be hot water."

But Frankie shook her head, and while I brushed my hair and teeth, she just rinsed off her arms and face in the sink. She was avoiding looking in the mirror.

We both walked back to our bedroom together.

"Are we safe here?" I asked, laying down on my bunk as soon as I'd pulled on a pair of sweats. I knew I'd be dreaming about monsters and was grateful that Lucifer was curling up behind my legs as I hid under the covers.

Frankie didn't say anything though, and I was asleep before I got an answer.

I went to school the next morning, though how I managed to talk myself out of playing sick and just hiding under my covers was beyond me. My folks would have let me stay. I never played sick. But I needed something normal after a decidedly not normal night.

I spent a long time in my journal, writing out the facts of what had happened the night before so I could do my best to keep them organized in my head.

We should have probably just locked ourselves up in the house, barred the doors, all that. But simultaneously, I didn't feel fear like I thought I should. It felt safe to get out into the daylight, and when I woke up from probably the hardest I've slept in my life, the sunlight streaming through the curtains was the most affirming thing I'd felt in a long time.

I grabbed an easy breakfast and half a cup of coffee.

"Late night?" Mom sat at the kitchen table reading the newspaper.

"Yeah, something like that." It occurred to me that I could tell her everything, but then something stopped me. The impulse was to stay quiet about it. A whisper in the back of my head nudging me to solve this on my own. To take care of this problem on my own.

I gave her a kiss on the cheek and took an apple off the table.

I went through my morning routine, including shaking Frankie awake. She groaned like she had been the last few days but sat up and at least told me that she wasn't going to school.

I flopped back on my bed, considering giving in to the soft sheets.

But I had a math quiz. And I would rather eat mud than ask my calculus teacher for a makeup date.

There is a burning feeling in your chest that you cannot quite place.

Water surrounds you, and when you stretch out your hands, metal bars the way. The metal bars are cold, and the water is cold.

The ache in your chest grows to a scream, and moving quickly away from the bars, you push backward and break out of the water. Taking in a labored breath, the bursting in your chest doesn't happen.

Not a bit of light reaches this place. You would rather leave, but there is something nagging at the base of your neck. Something you have to finish first. It will help.

But who will it help?

Turning a quarter of the way around, you take in a deep breath and dive into the water. You do not want to swim. You have to swim.

Chapter 25

I rolled out of bed for the second time that morning and shoved my textbooks into my bag. Then glancing at my bedside table, I tossed the flashlight and my water bottle into the bag as well.

Before I left, I unplugged Frankie's phone from the charging station across the room and handed it to her.

"If anything happens, call or text me." I put it firmly in her hand.

She opened up one eye from underneath her hoodie. "But you'll be in class."

"Anything, Frankie. Anything."

She nodded and rolled back over so she was facing the wall.

Closing our bedroom door quietly behind me, I grabbed a couple of granola bars and headed out.

When I got outside, I gave Byron a call, and he met me out at the sidewalk. "You look terrible," he said by way of greeting. Coming from anyone else, it would have felt completely rude, but he said it in his kind Byron way.

"I had a long night." I hadn't realized how anxious I was about actually telling anyone about what had happened until I felt the words trying to push their way out of my throat.

I could tell he was watching me to see if I was going to say more. I took a breath. With Byron, I knew I didn't have to hide when I was doing purposeful breathing, but part of me still was conditioned to mask my anxiety.

We waited for Sam for a few minutes, but it did not surprise me that he didn't come out of his house. We walked along in silence for a few yards.

"Just us today?" he asked, brow furrowed.

"Looks like." I shifted my backpack from one shoulder to the other.

"You know you really should wear your backpack evenly. Otherwise you'll get a shoulder ache." Byron said it so nonchalantly but with such subtle and genuine concern for my well-being that I almost burst into tears.

I drew in what was an audibly shaky breath and looked at him.

"Something really bad happened last night." I bit my lip, wondering if I was going to be brave enough to elaborate.

He didn't push me, just nodded and put his hand lightly on my upper arm.

"You can tell me when you're ready." He said it so kindly.

I didn't know if anyone had ever deserved a friendship so pure.

"I don't know how long it can wait." And I spilled. I told him everything that had happened with Sam and Jack and the deer and Mojito and whatever was creeping around in the forest. I told him about Frankie acting so strange and the email from the parents of the kids who were in the freak flood. And about the film Lyla and I had developed and how strange it was.

By the time I was done, he had sat me down on the sidewalk halfway to school and had me put my head between my knees so I could breathe.

"Right, well, that is a lot." He rubbed my back while I drew in deep breaths and nodded.

"Yeah, it's a lot."

"Have you told your parents?" He knew we were close and that I told them everything.

"I swear every time I try to, something stops me. It's the same with Frankie. She seems to have no idea what is going on half the time and the other half like she can't remember."

"Hmm."

"We should get to school." I stood up with his help and dusted off the butt of my jeans.

"You sure you want to go to school?" He looked me up and down, and I sighed.

"I just don't care. I want a class schedule and my locker."

"Can't take the nerd out of Jean."

This was an assessment I felt happy to lean into.

When we got to school and headed toward first period, I kept my eyes peeled for Lyla.

"Meet up for lunch?" Byron asked, giving my hand a squeeze. I nodded. "Definitely. I'm going to invite Lyla to eat with us."

"Sounds good. I'll see you in calc."

I hadn't decided whether I was going to spill everything to Lyla or not, but when I saw her walking up to me in the hallway between our first two classes, I knew I would.

"Hey." She had both hands looped around her backpack straps, and it was so '90s-movie cute I briefly considered ignoring the absolute disaster of a life I was living and just giving her googly eyes the rest of the day.

But she was helping me with the photographs, and I had some hunch-adjacent ideas I wanted to look into.

"Hi." I glanced down the hallway to see who all was around us. Everyone seemed subdued today.

"Where's your sister?" Lyla asked. "She wasn't in class. Our teacher said something about maybe a flu going around?"

I nodded. My own teacher had made a similar comment in my first hour. We had five students absent, which was quite a few, especially so close to midterms and progress reports.

"I don't think it's a flu." I hesitated, and she seemed to sense that.

"Is everything okay?" Concern furrowed her brow.

I shook my head, not wanting to have a second breakdown so early in the day. "No. But can we talk about it at lunch?"

"Of course." She put her arm on mine and gave it a gentle squeeze.

"Yearbook room?" I didn't want to chat in the cafeteria or quad where someone might overhear us. I was already so stressed out about even my best friends knowing what I was saying. I didn't want rumors to spread that I was spiraling. Even if that was what was going on.

The next two class periods felt like a million years, but finally Byron, Lyla, and I were in the yearbook offices, picking at our lunches. I hastily filled Lyla in on the previous night while she sat jaw dropped and her cafeteria burger untouched on her tray.

Near tears when I finished, I had to ask. "Do you believe me?"

It came out choked, but Lyla immediately slid her hand across the small desk and took mine in hers.

"Hey, look at me." She gave my hand a firm squeeze. "I believe you. Of course I do."

My relief was almost palpable enough to burst me into tears again, but I took in a breath and squeezed her hand back.

"Meara, Frankie, Sam, Blakely, and, like, a ton of other kids are all out today." Byron ticked them off on his fingers between bites of his veggie wrap. We were trying to figure out who all was missing from school because all of us had noticed more than just our friends were absent.

"It definitely seems like a lot more than usual. And it's not flu season or anything." I was quickly giving up on eating my sandwich and skipped to my cottage cheese comfort food.

"Or senior skip," Byron added then paused. "Unless it is and no one invited us."

I rolled my eyes. "I truly do not think that's what is happening. I'm on the Senior Sunrise committee, so skip day is scheduled already."

"Any idea what's going on? Are we going to address the big swamp monster issue?" Lyla held her arms out in a that-sort-of-seems-like-the-biggest-part sort of way.

"It would be weird if those two things weren't connected, right?" Byron wrapped up his sandwich, giving up on it for now. None of our appetites were great.

I nodded. "I agree. It doesn't make sense that suddenly everyone is acting weird, and Sam and Jack are getting captured by boogie monsters or whatever it is."

"Did Sam even say why he'd gone there?" Byron asked, and I shook my head.

"Sam was really fuzzy-headed and didn't really understand what had happened. It's like they were sleepwalking. I had to shake them awake over and over." I shuddered and unconsciously glanced at the window, double-checking that the sun was still up.

"What about Jack? Could he tell you where he'd been the last twenty hours?"

Again, I shook my head. "He was in no condition to answer questions at all. I only know he's alive at home because I texted him, like, seven times until he answered this morning."

The three of us sat there quietly for a few moments.

"What are we supposed to do?" Lyla asked. But not in the way that would indicate she felt like we were helpless. More like asking *me* what we were supposed to do.

"Well, option one," I said, "assume we're living on a hellmouth and just take our losses and move along with our families."

"And the second option, since none of our parents seem to even know anything is happening long enough to pack?" Byron tilted his head.

"Option two: assume we're living on a hellmouth and see if we can find a way to close it."

"Okay, Jean. So, we go with option two. Now what?" Lyla looked at me so earnestly I melted just a tad.

"I have two ideas," I said. They both looked at me expectantly. "One is we don't go anywhere alone and we come up with like some sort of text chain to make sure no one is sleepwalking."

They nodded, and I went on.

"Second, remember those photos we developed the other day?"

Lyla nodded.

"I think I'm having a hunch."

Chapter 26

Lyla and I showed Byron the negatives for the photos I thought might hold a clue about what was happening and who it was happening to. The one we'd developed of Meara and Frankie in the pipe was the first one we examined more closely. The fuzzy haze around them seemed to take shape as we looked at it.

"Do you think that's the swamp monster?" Lyla asked, tracing the lines around that half of the photograph.

I shrugged. "I didn't get a look at it. Quite purposefully. But it was big. I know that."

When we looked at the negatives, a similar lack of focus was around Meara and Frankie in all the photos after the one in the pipe.

Byron held the image up to the light. "It could definitely be something. Should we go get more photos?"

"Of what exactly?" Lyla asked.

"Well, if this was only happening to Frankie and Meara, I'd say just of them," he said. "But maybe we should go take a picture of Sam and Jack?"

I nodded. "There is definitely something happening with them, and whatever drew them to the woods or took them is obviously related."

My twenty-minute timer on my watch went off, and I shot a group text, making Sam, Meara, and Frankie check in. I kept the reason vague, just mentioning that I was worried since they were home sick.

They all obliged. Luckily for their sake and my anxiety, they responded quickly, even if it was with eye rolling emojis.

Lyla was sifting through the stack of images we had developed. "This all started at that pipe, right? When it burst during your clean up?"

"No, Frankie started acting weird before that," Byron pointed out. "Remember at the park when she swore she saw something? That was before the pipe."

I nodded. "You're right. So, if this is all related, it started for Frankie before the pipe. But everyone else after."

"Want to go take some photos there now, before it gets dark? We could make it back in time to print them this afternoon."

Normally, I would immediately say no to the thought of skipping out on a class, but it did make sense to do so right now. With all the kids out sick, we'd be easy to miss, and the pipe was close by.

"Okay, yeah." I grabbed my backpack and slung my camera around my neck, loading it with a fresh roll of film and pocketing another just in case we needed it.

"You sure you're all right doing this?" Byron furrowed his brows at me, but I nodded.

"I'd rather face it head on and figure out what is happening than stand around and do nothing." With a click, I double-checked that my flashlight was working and tucked it into my back pocket. "I don't like my friends being in danger."

"All right then, let's go." Byron held the door as we slipped out of the darkroom and used an emergency exit that we knew wouldn't sound any alarm, and took off around the back side of the school heading toward the drainage pipes.

"Hey, I should take your pictures too, probably." I raised the camera up and pointed it at Byron. "Say cheese."

"This is horrifying." He shook his head and gave me a smirk.

"Me next." Lyla struck a pose and winked at me.

"Okay, let's go." I clicked my lens cap back on.

"What about you?" Lyla asked, gesturing at the camera.

"What about me?" I kept walking.

"We need to get your photo too," she said.

"Oh, right." I unlooped my camera and handed it to her. "You know how to use it?"

She laughed. "I know my way around a camera."

Byron raised his eyebrow at me from behind her. We were definitely flirting...probably.

I had no idea how one was supposed to pose for a photograph that might show a shadow of doom upon development, but I managed anyway. Where are arms even supposed to go? Why was I so impossibly bad at taking up space that made sense?

As soon as that awful moment was over, we trudged forward, glancing backward every once in a while to make sure a random counselor hadn't decided to follow us off school property.

I couldn't help but look toward Stonefish Creek as we walked. It kept to my left, but all three of us were watching out of the corners of our eyes. I kept expecting to see movement, but the trees stayed as gentle and quiet as they had ever been. If anything, the thought of wandering by the water seemed peaceful and pleasant.

For more than just one moment, I wondered again if I had been dreaming. If everything I was experiencing was something I could explain away like Scrooge and his bit of mustard in *A Christmas Carol*. Maybe I ate something bad. Or mixed up my daytime meds with my nighttime ones.

I stopped walking, and Lyla and Byron stopped too.

"You okay?" he asked, stepping back to where I'd stopped.

"Nope." My voice quaked, and I was getting tired of feeling so emotionally out of control. I handed my camera to Lyla and pulled my backpack around so I could reach the little pillbox at the front of my bag. I dug out an emergency med and popped it in. They didn't require water, and I pulled in several breaths.

"You okay?" Byron asked again, and I nodded.

"I will be soon." I took another breath and turned my head to stare directly at the woods. It was still just the trees. The trees I'd grown up around and playing in and chasing Frankie and building forts.

The whiplash of wanting to go hang out in the woods swinging to absolute dread was getting to me.

Maybe I should direct my scared-shitless attitude into anger because I couldn't spend a relaxing freaking afternoon looking at the clouds through the leaves. I was leaving for college soon and had plans for these woods. They were going to be a clean and safe space for all the neighborhood kids, dang it.

I managed to give Byron and Lyla a thumbs-up, and grabbing Byron's hand, I stood back onto my feet.

"Let's go take some photos," I said.

We got to the pipe, and I peered through the opening, Byron and Lyla each looking over a shoulder.

"Here." Lyla handed me the print of the photo of Frankie and Meara with plans to line it up as best we could to see if we could recreate the effect from before.

I lifted the camera to my eye and snapped a photo, trying to line up the frame with the image as accurately as possible.

"Should we go closer?" I asked, crouched down and squinting into the dark. It was full daylight, but there were still eerily cast shadows up and down the pipe. The gaping hole from where the pipe had burst was bent and partially visible.

"Are you up for that?" Byron swallowed loudly.

"Let's go," I said.

The three of us scramble crawled through the ribbed metal, and I reminded myself to breathe. I pulled out the flashlight when we reached the opening.

There wasn't much to see other than darkness and dirt.

"Is that blood?" Lyla pointed at the jagged opening where the water had pushed through the wall. I pointed my light to it, and based on my vast knowledge from my first aid badge, I agreed that it did look like blood.

"How far back do you think it goes?" Byron used the light on his cell phone to aim it, but none of us could see much past what looked like a turn in the tunnel.

"I'm going in a little farther." I got onto my knees and crawled forward.

"Be careful," Lyla whispered.

"I don't think that's a good idea." Byron sounded ready to bolt.

"I'm just going a bit more." I was listening carefully, and aside from the muffled sound of an occasional car driving over the road, there was little to hear other than our own breathing.

Moving through the opening, I made my way forward. The tunnel was not much smaller than the pipe, but I was way more worried about it collapsing since it was just tightly packed dirt. Small puddles of water were on the ground every few feet, and the squelching sound made me regret wearing shorts. Though getting mud out of my clothes was going to be an entire process, and I probably shouldn't have been focused on laundry worries right then.

I got to the spot where the light from my flashlight hit a branch in the tunnel. Hoping that if something was lurking, it would have made itself known by then, I swung the light to the left and made myself look.

"There's just more dirt," I called back over my shoulder.

"Okay, then come on back," Lyla called.

I began backing up, but then I heard a sound.

It took me a minute to figure out what I was hearing.

It was gurgling and bubbling but not like the squelching the monster had made. This was more like water boiling but thicker.

The sound was close by. Close enough that I wanted to at least check it out.

"I'm gonna go a little farther," I called.

I edged forward a bit more and hit another corner. But the sound was getting louder, and I wanted to see what was making it.

When I moved around the corner, my hand slipped, and I landed on my stomach. Whatever was on the ground was not mud, and a metallic smell hit me. I got back onto my knees and pointed the flashlight ahead.

Instead of a tunnel, I was looking down on a large opening about the size of a couple of school buses. The burbling sound was coming from the bottom, and I could see from where I kneeled that it was dark and slick like whatever I had slipped in.

Swinging my backpack to where I could reach the plastic water bottle I'd grabbed from the recycling on our way here, I uncapped it and made my way downward with the hopes of snagging a water sample. The sides were slippery, but there were tree branches I could hold onto, and I held my flashlight in my teeth. Lowering myself down, I dipped my water bottle into the liquid, trying to keep it off my hands.

I climbed back up to the exit when I noticed part of a cement wall partially covered by dirt and what looked like it might be a sign of some sort. There was also a pile of something like clutter from a construction site. Using the roots, I walked sideways a few yards to the sign and pushed off the rest of the dirt so I could see what it said.

I expected something like "hazardous waste site, get the heck out, you're gonna grow three extra eyes," but it was just a company name. It sounded vaguely familiar, but I couldn't place it. Instead, I took a photo, hoping it would be clear enough for us to look it up later.

Then I scrambled out and set my camera on the longest exposure available, setting it on top of my backpack to hold it steady while I took several photos of the hole as best I could.

I turned and began crawling out, when the gurgling and slurping sound seemed to get louder. I wasn't sure if it was my imagination or not, but I crawled a lot faster out than I'd gone in.

"Is something behind you?" Byron asked as I scurried out of the hole.

"I don't think so, but let's get out of here anyway. Sound good?" I was out of breath and beginning to worry I was developing claustrophobia.

"Works for me," Lyla agreed, and the three of us exited the pipe as quickly as we could.

Chapter 27

We got back to school right before fifth period, and I swore I would make a terrible rebel. I quickly tossed my dirty clothes into my gym locker and borrowed a sweatshirt from Lyla. When the coach popped in and asked how my day was going, I almost blurted out an apology for running away before we'd even reached any sort of situation where I might have to explain where I'd been. By the end of fifth, all three of us had convinced our respective teachers that we should be allowed to head to the yearbook room and make better use of our time. Most teachers were just doing study hours anyway because so many students were absent.

So before the school day had even ended, the three of us stood around the negatives stretched long and narrow on the back light.

"I think we should just print them all." Byron stood with his arms crossed, peering over Lyla's and my shoulders while we worked.

Just as I rolled my eyes a bit, Lyla said, "That would take a really long time, so let's try to focus on the ones that we think are the most telling?"

We'd already spent a good fifteen minutes scrolling through Byron's cell phone photographs, which either showed increasingly regular photos or blurrier and blurrier photos of us he'd taken in the pipe's dimness.

"Eventually, I would like it if you could take at least one good photo of me." I handed Byron back his cell phone. He'd been taking not super great photos of me since we were, like, eight years old, and this was no exception.

"How do we pick which ones to use?" He leaned over and squinted into the magnifying glass while he perused the strips of images.

"I think it's part gut, part luck?" Lyla said. "We're pretty new to this."

I liked how Lyla said "we."

"We definitely need to print the one with the sign. I feel like I've seen that logo somewhere." I said.

We spent the next few minutes choosing the images we would print out and got to work. It went quickly now that Lyla and I both had experience working in the darkroom. And Byron was always a quick study, so he was a big help as well.

On a hunch, I reprinted the one of Meara and Frankie that we'd developed before. "Whoa, look at this one."

We watched as the image developed. There was clearly something odd around Frankie and Meara both. In more clarity, some sort of black, fog-like tendrils reached between them, and it looked like it was stretching toward Sam, who was to the right in the frame.

"What is that?" Byron leaned in closer.

"I don't know, but it's all over the two of them. Look at this one." Lyla pointed to another photo, this one of me and Frankie together, and it almost looked like she was partly wrapped in long, wet strings.

"They're not touching you," Byron noted. He was right. Even though the two of us had our arms looped around each other in the photo, the tendrils didn't reach me.

"That is so weird." Lyla traced her finger along the line between me and Frankie. Like we should have been conjoined but were entirely separated.

"Y'all, look at this one though." My heart raced. It was a group photo taken at the second park cleanup day. Every other kid in the image had similar traces near or on them. I let out a breath I had been holding when I saw that neither Byron nor Lyla had any of the markings on them.

But Jack and Sam sure did. And a bunch of others.

"What do you want to bet the kids that have this stuff on them are the ones who are out sick?" Lyla shuddered and wrapped her arms around her chest.

Byron gave her a gentle pat on the shoulder. "I think you're right. I know at least three of them were gone this morning."

"This is getting scarier." I was breathing a bit harder than I should have been. "Let's get out of this room, okay?"

They both nodded, and we flipped on the lights and left. I was feeling claustrophobic and needed to sit down. I made it to the floor and put my back against the wall, popping off my shoes.

"What do you need?" Byron asked, kneeling down beside me.

"To not have a full-blown panic attack right now?" I smiled weakly. I truly did not have time to deal with another, though historically telling myself that did not a calm Jean make.

"Here, have some water." Lyla handed me my emotional support water bottle.

I took small sips and rubbed my thumb up and down the calm strip.

"I'm not going to tell you this is all gonna be okay." Byron sat next to me and took off his own shoes. I snorted. "Thanks for the vote of confidence."

He frowned at me. "You know this isn't your problem to solve alone, right, Jean?"

I shook my head. "It got bad when we were out cleaning up by that pipe. And Frankie is my sister. I have to protect her. The park is my project. I can't let anything happen to it. She needs me." The words seemed to just gush out of me in one long stream.

"Whoa, okay, take a breath." Lyla sat next to me and took my hand. "This is not all on you."

I wanted to believe them. But I swore I'd always watch out for Frankie. When she got sick, I promised myself and her that I'd always take care of her. Now something was happening to her and to our park. Something I was responsible for. It happened during my club's cleanup.

"Hey." Byron took my face gently in his hand. "You're spiraling. Let's shake off those intrusive thoughts. Have them. Let them go."

I nodded and closed my eyes.

Frankie might die. It was my fault. I held both thoughts like rocks in my brain then let them clatter down into a pile of other thoughts.

"Right," I said after a while had passed. My stomach had settled enough to nibble on the granola bar I'd brought and sip the orange juice Byron had produced out of his backpack. "Time to do some research."

191

The name in the pipe was Ranhills Construction Company. I knew that name sounded familiar. I turn the computer on, holding the image of the plaque. Byron took the seat next to me, studying the photo.

"Isn't that the name of the place we took a field trip a few years back?" He handed the photo to Lyla, who shrugged.

"I just moved here." She was riffling through the other photos. "And frankly, I've not had much time to go sightseeing."

"I'll take you," I offered. Maybe a bit too eagerly, I wasn't sure. Was the middle of what felt like the end of the world the best time to ask someone cute to go on a make up field trip with you?

"It's a date." She smiled and nodded to the computer that had booted up.

I turned away, blushing, and opened the browser, typing in a few search terms.

At first, nothing much came up. The Ranhills Estate and all their companies had been around for ages, and they had done the most recent construction addition to the north of the park and our neighborhood. Pretty basic suburban sprawl.

But when I added the term "monster," the search led to something much different.

Headlines on several blogs offered a lot of information.

"Construction workers scared to return to work because of swamp monster," read one site.

"That could be our dude." Byron pointed to the description.

"Unbelievably large and with glowing green eyes? I don't think it's eyes were glowing."

"Well, this is a blog about someone who hunts for Bigfoot full time so might not be the most accurate information." Lyla pointed to the thumbnail and picture of the author.

"It says here that the swamp thing has been spotted in a lot of places around Oklahoma. Look." I clicked on the map icon. "There's a map."

"I love a good map," Byron said.

I gave him a high five without looking. "Same."

"You two are nerds." Lyla laughed and turned on the other computer. "I guess more than one of us can be searching."

The map showed several spots around Oklahoma, but it was just a photograph of a paper map that had been uploaded, so we couldn't click on any of the spots.

Lyla was on it though and pulled up Google Maps on her computer.

"Genius." Byron smiled at her.

Using the computer program, we compared the map on the website to the satellite images. Sure enough, there was one right on top of our park. The others were scattered around Eastern Oklahoma and Western Arkansas.

"This one is in Fouke, Arkansas." I pointed to another mark that was circled. Further googling and we discovered a documentary from the '70s that we could stream.

"That seems similar to our monster, but is ours ape-like?" Byron noted after we skimmed the information about that particular creature. "Does this mean we get to name it?"

"What would you call it?" Lyla asked.

"Seems like something we would need to workshop." Byron walked over to the whiteboard and wrote down words like "swamp" and "creature" and "monster."

"Is now really the time to be doing that?" I put in another search, specifically adding construction sites to it to see if I could find more information about the incidents.

"I think it's the perfect time." Lyla got up too. She walked into the darkroom briefly and returned with several photos and some tape. She put them up on the board where Byron was writing and added a few arrows and descriptions, like "enjoys the outdoors" and "reeks to high heaven."

I continued to find articles, but this time I printed them out as I did. I could get on board with an old-school detective setup.

"This comment calls it a 'low budget Bigfoot.'" Lyla tacked the printout up on the board.

"Well, that's rude." I wasn't totally sure why I was getting defensive, but I was. "There is nothing low budget about our swamp thing."

Byron, Lyla, and I stood staring at the whiteboard and printouts posted across it.

Before we knew it, the final bell was ringing, and we had moved into the darkroom to pin things up on the walls in a place where the custodians and teachers wouldn't mind because it was out of sight.

We'd scoured the internet for instances of a creature like ours, and while many of the sites were—shall we say—dubious, it felt like we were on the right track.

"But don't creatures like Bigfoot stick to areas with way more space? Like the skunk one we read about from Florida. It's on a million acres of swamp. And the yeti is always in giant mountain ranges." Byron had printed out a map of the world and was busy pushing pins into locations where those creatures chose to appear.

"What if it's only here because something made it come out of something like a hibernation?" I was racking my brain for what could have caused it to appear so suddenly. "I've spent, like, my whole life in that park and never run into anything like this. You too, Byron."

"Seems like it would have been hard to miss," Lyla agreed.

I nodded. "We would have noticed for sure. So, something must have changed."

"Back to the water pipe explosion again." Byron tapped his index finger on the timeline we'd cobbled together as best we could, and most things pointed to that moment. "It's got to have something to do with that and the construction company."

"But what caused the pipe to burst, and what does it have to do with the construction? It wasn't anything like sewage that came out of the ground. It was definitely water." Lyla noted. "And we haven't noticed any oil slicks or anything, right?"

I remembered the bottle of water and pulled it out of my bag, thinking it might have some indication of oil, but it was definitely not black or oily.

"Why is it so green?" Byron peered at the water bottle.

The inside of it was water that was *green* green. Kermit the Frog on a sunny end of the rainbow day green.

"I guess algae, but that wouldn't make a pipe burst." Lyla held the bottle in her hand for a moment before passing it back to me.

"Could have been an earthquake that caused it," Byron suggested.

"We would have felt that, right?" I felt like there was something we were missing.

"What do we think the swamp thing is trying to do?" Lyla asked, and for the first time, I thought about that.

"I'm not sure. It seems to be bringing kids to it, but why?" Byron looked thoughtful.

"I don't know," I said, "but we need to find out soon. I can't spend so many sleepless nights rescuing folks. Eventually whatever it is might start affecting all of us."

The object in your hand is the size of your palm, and it vibrates, registering as a signal in your brain, but you do not pay it much mind.

Smooth tile floors stretch out in front of you. Metal cabinets line both sides of the tunnel you are in.

Lights flicker brightly. Finding a switch, you flick it, and the glare deadens. You prefer it to be dark. The brightness was painful.

Like most places you find yourself, this one is familiar.

There is something you are looking for. Someone you are looking for.

Voices drift from down the tunnel.

It's a hallway, not a tunnel.

Your hand touches one of the metal boxes.

It's your locker. It belongs to you.

Following the voices, you shuffle closer, feet steady as your boots echo off the tile.

Chapter 28

"Okay, but if the swamp thing is mad about the construction or whatever, what are we supposed to do about it?" Byron frowned.

"And why is it attacking kids? I don't get that either." Lyla rubbed her hand over her face.

"The stories about it appearing all seem to stop when the construction site is closed and the area is cleaned up." I was staring at the timeline we'd made. Most of the information was from blogs about cryptids, but we were going to have to use what we could find.

"So, we clean up the area." Byron held his hands out, palms up, as though it were the simplest thing in the world.

"That's literally what we were doing when it took Jack and Sam. We were literally cleaning up the area. In the *literal* literal sense." I was frustrated. I had poured so much energy into protecting the park, and now we were going to have to, like, call in the Ghostbusters to get rid of this thing.

"Okay, but if you're the monster, how would that look to you?" Lyla tilted her head, and I could practically see a lightbulb flickering on over top of her.

"What do you mean?" Byron asked.

"Well," she said, "if I had been underground or wherever for fifty years and popped up to a bunch of teenagers carrying giant bags of garbage in big, plastic contractor bags, I might not know what they were there for."

"You're onto something, I think." It was clicking for me too. "We were in a huge group with tons of trash on us. If it wants to clean up the park, it would see the trash as the biggest threat."

"And the teenagers who were carrying the litter," Byron added.

"Plus," Lyla said, "when it took Sam, he'd left with all the bags that we'd already filled. Then with all the worry about Jack, we left quite a few. We knew we'd finish cleaning them up, but the monster wouldn't."

"Can it be as simple as that though?" Byron frowned.

"The US alone produces over three million tons of plastic bag waste every year, according to the EPA," I said. "So I could see it."

"Jean, you just had that number in your head?" Lyla gave me what I was going to consider an adoring look.

I blushed. "I tried to get the environmental club sponsors to let us use compostable ones. The trash still ends up in a landfill if it's not recycled, but at least then the bags wouldn't add to it. But they're super expensive."

"So, it really could be that," Byron said excitedly.

"Okay, so we're saying the swamp monster is snagging kids because those kids are carrying around bags of trash and it's confusing that for the cause of the trash?" Lyla summarized.

I shrugged. It was a better theory than any we had come up with, and it sort of made sense. I hated the litter in the park so much that I'd started a whole cleanup program. If this creature wanted to protect the park, then it might do whatever it could too. Was I really relating to a teen-stealing swamp monster? Did we...get each other?

"But how do we stop the swamp thing without getting eviscerated? I really don't want to wind up as erosion goop." Byron shuddered.

"By the way, before we run off to buy compostable trash bags, are we sticking with Swamp Thing?" Lyla squinched up her nose. "I know I keep harping on this, but it would be nice to be consistent."

"Is Swamp Thing really an option? It's kinda taken, right?" Byron frowned.

"I was using it as a common noun and a pronoun. As in a thing in the swamp. I don't care what we call it." I shrugged.

"How about the Nature Park Ripper?" Lyla threw out there.

Which made me realize I actually did care about what we called it and almost jumped in until Byron did.

"Right, well, that doesn't make any sense." Byron wrote it down anyway. We'd begun the brainstorming act with one of those "no bad ideas" mentalities. Though some of the ideas were decidedly bad.

"It did kinda rip up that deer though?" Lyla wrinkled her nose.

"How about we call it the Legend of Stonefish Creek?" I suggested.

"That's kind of a mouthful," Byron said, and I threw up my hands.

"We could go the route of, like, Nessie. Doesn't have to be a big formal one." Lyla added.

"Let's put a pin in that for now and focus on what we're gonna do about it. I don't think I'm gonna care we didn't have a name figured out when it's dissolving my insides. Or drowning me in monster hair." As much as I love a good title, I was more focused on the attacking part.

"Going on the trash bag theory, that explains one thing, but what made the monster show up in the first place? There has to be something to do with the construction." Lyla pointed out.

"I think we need to keep looking into it. There are so many types of pollution. Maybe we're just not seeing it," Byron said. "Let's go home and regroup."

I nodded. "Lyla and I will get Frankie. You get Meara. We know they're connected to the swamp thing in some way, and we might be able to use them to speak to it."

"Sounds good. We'll meet back up in, say, an hour? At your house?" Byron pulled on his backpack, and Lyla and I did the same.

We were about to go when a sudden noise made all three of us jump.

We turned toward the door leading to the classroom.

"Is it locked?" Lyla whispered, and I shook my head.

Moving as steadily as I could, I pushed the door to the darkroom closed. From across the dim room, the lights had mostly been turned off when the teacher left us to work, but we could see the door to the classroom jump when whoever—or whatever—it was pounded once, twice, three times.

With shaking hands, I slid the small lock on the door and almost tripped on a stool as I backed up. Byron flipped off the light, plunging us into darkness a moment before we heard the classroom door slam open. As though all the air was pulled out of the room, the three of us held a collective breath, straining so hard to listen it felt like the world had gotten the volume turned all the way down.

Then a shuffling sound came in from the hallway. It sounded like something being dragged across the floor. Whoever was doing it was breathing audibly, like they were having to exert themselves.

With a thump that made us all jump and Lyla grab my hand, something dropped onto the linoleum classroom floor.

I bit my lip to keep the yelp building up in my throat down.

Which was made even more difficult when something started scratching at the door to the darkroom. It was soft at first, like nails slowly trailing down a textured wall.

Then it pounded again. A loud rap that vibrated the door on its hinges.

All three of us jumped involuntarily, and someone knocked what sounded like a stack of photo paper onto the floor. It landed with a snap, and the room outside the closet got deathly silent.

I was sure we were mincemeat. Then I wondered what mincemeat was. And whether it was "mince" or "minced." Either way, I was certain we were going to be dissolved into a mud puddle or made into monster pie.

Then a cell phone rang.

For a second, I thought it belonged to one of us, but it was coming from the other side of the door.

It rang again, and the undeniable sound of "Rebel Girl" echoed through the door.

"Is that Bikini Kill?" Lyla breathed, barely over a whisper.

I nodded then realized she couldn't see me. Giving her hand a squeeze, I let go and walked toward the door. As I stepped away, she tugged at my arm.

"Jean, no," she whispered.

"It's okay."

I went to the door and whispered, "Frankie, is that you?"

But the only response we got was something on the other side jiggling the handle.

"Don't," both Byron and Lyla whispered as I unlocked the door and pulled it open.

Frankie was there.

Her cellphone gripped in her hand, she was shaking and looked feverish like she had when I'd left her at home.

"Frankie, what is it?" I rushed toward her, but she put up a hand to stop me at arm's length.

"What the actual hell, Frankie," Byron said. He and Lyla stood wide-eyed in the darkroom. He glared at her, and Lyla's mouth was open.

"You scared the crap out of us," Lyla added.

But Frankie didn't respond to either of them. She dropped something from her other hand, and it clattered to the floor.

"That's my phone." I bent and scooped it up. Flipping open the screen, I could see Frankie's number was up, and a voicemail was recording on my end.

Byron and Lyla both stepped forward into the classroom, looking around as if they expected to see something or someone else in addition to Frankie.

But the classroom was empty except for us.

"What's going on, Frankie?" I asked, trying to get a read on her.

Her jaw was tensed, clamped shut. Her hands kept opening and closing into fists. I took a tentative step closer, and she stepped back the smallest amount.

"Frankie, you have to let me help you." I stretched my hand toward her, but she stepped just out of reach again.

Then her eyes moved to the whiteboard where we'd been collecting our information about the creature. For a moment, her eyes widened and then narrowed, and she blinked them closed, turning away from the collage of newspaper and blog clippings.

"Talk to me, Frankie." I was trying not to beg or cry or both. But I needed to help her. I needed her to tell me what to do and I would do it. I'd do whatever she needed me to.

So, when she turned abruptly and walked to the exit, I didn't hesitate and grabbed my backpack to follow her, Byron and Lyla close on my heels.

Chapter 29

"Where are we going?" Byron asked.

He, Lyla and I hurried to keep up with Frankie. She wasn't running, but she was focused on a direct path and stepping through bushes and over curbs to reach it. Going through the nearly empty parking lot of the school, she didn't even move out of the line of cars, clipping her arm on a side mirror, which luckily was one that kicked in and out on purpose so, though the sound was jarring, I hoped it would not bruise her too badly.

"I think we're heading to the pipe." Byron pointed straight ahead.

I agreed. If we kept going this direction, we'd be there soon too. I was not keen on reentering it and was a bit relieved when Frankie headed over the embankment.

"What's the plan, Jean?" Lyla asked. The three of us were breathing hard to keep up with Frankie, who was acting like she'd been training to climb Mount Everest.

"We follow her and see what happens next." I panted, and my voice came out shaky.

Frankie was headed straight toward something.

My stomach dropped when she began marching across the street, not looking left or right. A Jeep swerved out of the way just in time before hitting her and laid on its horn, the sound making the other three of us jump.

But Frankie continued to ignore everything around her.

We all got safely the rest of the way across and Frankie leaned down, pulling up a grate that I'd never seen before but must have connected to the rest of the pipes.

All of us made to follow her, but she put an arm out and spoke for the first time. "Just Jean."

"No way." Lyla stepped up next to me and put her hand on my shoulder protectively.

"Absolutely not," Byron agreed, and while I loved them both dearly for it, I knew I was going to do whatever Frankie said.

"I think we need to listen to her." I took out my headlamp and slung it over my neck.

"Listen to her?" Byron hissed. "She's not even talking. How are we supposed to listen to her?"

"Just trust me," I pleaded. "You two go home and check on Meara and Sam and the others. We have to find a way to get rid of whatever this thing is, so keep looking into it. I'll be back as soon as I figure out what Frankie is doing. It will hopefully help us figure out what we need to do about the swamp thing."

"You do realize this is absolutely probably a trap, right?" Lyla took my hand, and was practically begging me with her pretty eyes not to go. "What if you get hurt or worse?"

But my mind was made up. "Frankie wouldn't let anything happen to me," I whispered back. "Think about last night. I was fine, right?"

"If we're using 'fine' in the loosest sense of the word." Byron crossed his arms, scowling.

Frankie stood at the mouth of a tunnel I'd never seen before, but I guessed it led underground to an area like the space we'd found earlier.

"I don't think that's totally Frankie, Jean," Byron whispered warily.

But I shook my head. "Even if it's not totally her, it's still her. I believe that with all my heart, and I'm going to find out what she needs me to do."

"Promise us you'll run if you have to," Lyla said, and Byron nodded in agreement.

"I promise. And you promise you'll go find out the rest of what we need. We have to make sure Sam and Meara are safe."

They nodded reluctantly and gave me quick hugs.

"Now. Jean." Frankie's voice was gravelly.

I swallowed hard. "Coming, Frankie."

Byron and Lyla didn't leave until I was out of sight, and looking back one last time, I gave them some finger guns because despite, being in a life-or-death situation, I was still an absolutely smooth person who was great at knowing what to do with my hands.

I followed her into the pipe. It was similar to the one that had burst, but this one was intact, if still rusty and grimy. We crouched and crawled through it until we came to a T in the system. I was grateful that I'd brought my head lamp and worn pants that were already garbage.

Though I made a mental note to invest in some waders. A thought occurred to me that maybe when we all made it through this, Lyla would like to go thrift store shopping with me.

To the right was a dead end after about three feet. There was a solid wall of concrete, and then the pipe just ended abruptly. A grate above the space let in slants of afternoon light, and for a moment, we didn't need my headlamp.

The other side was the same, and I pointed it out. "It's a dead end, Frankie."

She let out a half grunt as a response and crouched down at the bottom of one wall. Then, finding seams I hadn't even noticed, she pushed her fingers into a crack and pulled a chunk of the wall out, revealing a crawl space about the size of a sewer hole cover.

Which was full of water.

She nodded toward it.

I did not understand. Or at least I didn't want to understand.

"Frankie, no." I shook my head. I wasn't going in.

But she still wasn't listening to me any more than she had been before.

Dropping her cell phone on the rock she'd moved away from the wall, she turned her face toward me, her expression blank. Except her eyes were watering.

"The water is deep enough." Her voice came out croaking and harsh but quiet.

"Frankie, what does that mean?" I wanted to grab her by the shoulder and beg her to tell me what was going on. I wanted to drag her back the way we'd come and take her to a doctor. I wanted to force her to talk to me. To tell me what she needed me to do to help her break out of whatever this was.

She didn't respond to my question though and instead held up a hand and moved up one finger at a time as though she was counting.

When she stopped, she looked at me.

"Fifteen?" I asked. "Fifteen what? What's fifteen?"

Then, not bothering to speak, she pinched her nose and took a deep breath. After watching me as though to make sure I was paying attention, she nodded once, turned, and dove into the water under the cement.

Her combat boots pushing off the base of the floor was the last bit of her I saw.

If it had been anyone else, maybe what I did next would have been different. Or I would have let the anxiety settle in and win and I'd have turned around and left. Or maybe I'd have just sat right down and had a full-blown panic attack on the dirty cement square until someone realized I was missing and sent out a search party.

But I *was* the search party.

And it was Frankie who had just disappeared into black depths.

She was going to owe me so many chores for this if we ever got out of it.

I closed my eyes and, laying flat on my belly, reached as far into the hole as I could, imagining all manner of icky things that might be lurking.

Cold, dark water was all I could feel at first. Stretching, I could make out the ridges of a metal pipe just where my fingers could reach. I spent what felt like way too many precious seconds, stretching toward the other sides, and sure enough, it was the same thing.

Assuming Frankie wasn't purposefully leading me to my death, I set my cell phone where she'd left hers, hoping it wasn't going to be all that remained of us. Shrugging off my jacket, I gave myself a full ten seconds to internally freak the heck out.

Then I held my breath and dove into the pitch-black water.

I counted down from fifteen in my head and broke the surface as I got to four.

My headlamp reflected against Frankie's back, where she sat out of the water on a small, muddy landing.

I pulled myself out and, crouching next to her, looked around.

The walls were the same metal and concrete as the other portions of the pipe, but there was also a large opening into the darkness behind where she sat. Below us, around five feet down, was an underground stream. I made a mental note to add water table to the list of things we needed to look up. The water flowed freely between low, grated openings on either side. I didn't want to think about what it would have felt like to hit a grate.

My light barely reached, but I could see that, across the flowing water, there was another small incline like the one we were sitting on and a larger opening beyond it.

I swiveled my light to Frankie, who was watching me take in the scene.

"Hey," she said quietly. For a second, she seemed to be herself.

"Frankie?"

She nodded, and I burst into tears and lunged toward her for a hug. She held me briefly then gently pushed me away.

"Come on." She turned and dropped down the side of the stream, standing on a narrow ledge of concrete along the side.

I took in a breath and swallowed my tears, following her. Turning on my belly, I resisted the urge to close my eyes as I dropped down the few inches. I almost lost my footing, but she grabbed my elbow, steadying us.

"Don't disturb the water." She held my gaze as she said it.

"That's a line from *Lord of the Rings*."

"I am no Gollum."

Shuffling with our backs to the water, I followed her to the other side. There, pieces of rebar stuck out from the wall and made a sort of horizontal ladder. She didn't seem to need the light but moved slowly enough that I kept up with her as we carefully made our way across the gap and stepped back onto concrete on the other side. Frankie held out her hand to me as I took the last steps off the ladder onto the other side.

"Steady" was all she said as she turned and climbed up the other side, using a similar metal ladder built into the wall.

I hadn't planned on speeding up to the top, but I was glad I had my headlamp because several of the rungs were either missing or, worse, broken off. Rusty metal tubing stuck out from the wall. I thought about the scrape I'd seen on Frankie's side and the tear in her sweater and shuddered.

"Steady," I whispered to myself as I caught up with her at the top of the ten-foot climb.

"Slippery," she said.

I was tired of only one-word explanations from her, but it was better than the silence.

She was right to warn me. The other side was slick, and when I put my hand down to touch it, whatever was making it slippery came up greasy and smooth in my hand. But it didn't smell industrial or metallic. There was a subtle, musty, decaying smell but not quite like what I'd smelled in the park or coming from that awful thing in our drain.

"It's so green." I looked more closely at the slickness. If it had been in the light, I would have called it neon. "Like Lisa Frank green."

Frankie waited for me to stop poking around, and we kept working our way toward the large opening.

"What is this?" I peered over the edge.

There was a large cavern below us, and I could see runoff from a plastic construction tube streaming into the water in the cavern. It was silty and looked like sand. The water here was clear.

"Close it." Frankie nodded to the open pipe.

I looked closer, realizing it had threads inside like part of a giant nut. I looked around but couldn't find whatever had gone into it previously. "Where's the lid or cap or whatever you call it?"

Frankie didn't say anything, just looked down at the muddy who-knew-how-deep puddle below where we stood.

"Great," I said. "Just absolutely fantastic."

Chapter 30

"Thank goodness." Lyla rushed toward me and Frankie as we opened the gate to our backyard.

Byron was waiting there too, but he hung back a smidge, as Lyla didn't hesitate to wrap her arms around me. After a beat, I let myself relax a fraction of a bit and lay my head on her shoulder.

"I'm getting you all soggy," I murmured, suddenly self-conscious about the state of disaster my clothes were in and simultaneously not caring even the slightest.

"We were so worried." She squeezed me close again and then let go, looking me up and down as though assessing whether I was in one piece.

"Frankie?" Byron looked at her quizzically. But I shook my head.

She was comatose but walking upright as I led her to our house.

"We need to get her inside and laid down." I motioned toward our back door.

The two of them followed me in, Byron taking Frankie gently by the elbow. Our parents weren't home from work yet, so we didn't have to hide the fact that we were half coated in slime and our clothes were a wreck.

When we got to our room, I had Byron and Lyla wait outside while I quickly got Frankie out of her clothes and into some sweats then laid her down on my bunk rather than try to figure out how to get her onto the top one. I pulled the curtains, though there was still afternoon sun pooling through the fabric, and by the time I turned back around, Frankie's eyes were closed, and she was breathing steadily.

I slipped out of our room and pulled the door partway shut.

"What do you need?" Lyla asked as the three of us stood in the hallway.

"You checked in with Meara and Sam?"

Byron and Lyla nodded.

"Then nothing. Well, I mean, I should shower, but I don't think we have time."

"What did you find out?" Byron asked.

"The cause of the pollution isn't oil, which makes sense since we didn't, like, see or smell anything like that." I regretted having spent so many minutes considering that to be the underlying issue, but there wasn't enough time to dwell on my inherent bias against big companies. Frankie had apparently rubbed off on me.

"What is it then?" Lyla asked.

"Nitrogen," I said.

"Huh?" Byron frowned. Then, bless his nerdy heart, he pulled out his chemistry textbook.

"Well, technically nitrates," I elaborated. "It's causing an algae bloom."

"I thought algae was, like, a normal water thing." Lyla's eyebrows did a cute little crease thing.

I nodded. "It is usually but only in the right amount. And right now, there is way too much." I sat down crisscross next to Byron in the hallway.

"Not using tables anymore, huh?" Lyla asked.

I couldn't help but laugh in my exhaustion. The thought of walking all the way downstairs about did me in, and I wanted to be as close to Frankie as I could and still talk to Byron and Lyla.

"Silt runoff from that new housing development is getting into the water table and causing an algae bloom." I pointed to the page Byron had just flipped to.

"Not all water pollution is caused by oils and garbage." He ran his finger down the page until he got to the portion about the negative effects of too many nitrates or phosphates in water ways.

"What's it doing to the water?" Lyla looked at the image of the algae bloom example in the book. Bright, unearthly green coated the entire pond.

"You weren't in Oklahoma yet, but last summer there was a really bad algae bloom at one of our lakes. It killed, like, half the fish that lived there and caused all sorts of problems with the dam and stuff." I pulled up some photos on Byron's phone and showed her.

There had been major damage to the Lake Hobotnica dam, and it was still being cleaned up.

"It was really awful," Byron added. "So many dead fish and other animals. And no one could swim in it because it was like a steamy bacteria lake. If you drank it accidentally, it made you really sick."

"And pets got sick too," I pointed out. "Maybe that's why Mo has been freaking out so much."

"Okay, but what can we do?" Lyla asked.

"Frankie and I found where the silt causing the algae bloom is coming from," I said. "And we capped it where it was leaking into the water."

"Then problem solved?" Lyla asked with jazz hands.

I chuckled. Jazz hands. "Not quite. We need to get the water moving at the other end again. When the pipe burst, it pushed everything away from the sides of the creek banks and caused a blockage."

"So, how do we do that?" Byron asked.

I took a piece of notebook paper out of my backpack and spread it out, drawing a quick sketch of the park.

"The most likely place the clog is happening is here." I pointed to where I'd drawn a series of circles in place of tubes. "They're pretty similar to the ones at the top of the drainage system. Because they're fairly far back off the trails, I haven't been monitoring them as much as the more common areas for the cleanup days."

"So, take some shovels and clear them out, and bada bing, bada boom, algae disappears, and swamp thing stops blaming the environmental club for ruining its day, lets everyone go, and scurries away." Byron summarized.

My instinct was to counter but… "I mean, yeah, that seems about right."

"One problem though," Byron said. "That thing definitely does not want us around it."

"Then we'll just have to be sneaky and fast." I glanced at the door to my bedroom.

"It's getting late." Lyla looked at her watch. "Should we wait until morning?"

I shook my head. "Whatever this thing is doing to Frankie and the others, I don't want to wait. We need to take care of this now." My anxiety would not settle for anything less than immediate action, even though my body was begging to curl up under ten inches of covers and put on some rug cleaning YouTube videos and just ignore the world for a solid week. But I thought about all of my friends who might be in danger. "Until we can convince this thing we're not here to hurt it, it's going to keep drawing folks to it."

Byron shuddered. "We don't want anyone to end up mush."

"Hard agree." I stood and reached a hand down to help Lyla up as well.

"I'll call our friends and see who I can get ahold of." Byron wagged his phone at us. "You two want to grab tools to fix the clog?"

"Works for me," I said. "You let me know if Frankie wakes up?"

Byron gave me a thumbs-up.

"Let's get to it." Lyla nodded.

We went downstairs and into the backyard together, making a beeline for the shed that stood at the back corner and was rarely used. It had a padlock on it, but we kept it unlocked, just hooked through the door latch. Removing the padlock, I opened up the wooden door and started sorting through supplies.

We ended up with a hoe, two rakes, a shovel, several spades, and a crowbar.

"Think this will be enough to clear the blockage?" Lyla asked, her arms full of gardening tools.

"It's a start at least." I continued to sift through the shed and produced several sets of gloves. "Though it might consider these things to be garbage, so we'll still want to move quickly, I think."

We piled up the tools in the back of the pickup and Lyla and Byron put on clothes that could get messy. On our way back to my bedroom, we stopped in at the kitchen to grab some protein.

"I feel like I haven't eaten in a week." I couldn't help but let out a satisfied noise as I bit into a quarter of a block of cheddar cheese that I'd cut off.

"Same," Lyla said, adding some snacks to a plate for Byron and Frankie as she scarfed down some salami and carrots. I opened a bottle of sweet tea and poured half into a glass then chugged the other half.

"Fighting swamp monsters will really build up your appetite." I winked in a very cool way as I said that.

But I was rewarded with a lopsided smile and Lyla saying, "I'll toast to that." We clinked our teas together and then both stood for a moment and caught our breath.

In the silence, I felt the throbbing doom that was possibly going to plop itself down on my life even more. Thoughts rushed into my head—my parents and Frankie and the park and my friends becoming absorbed and washed away with the silt and the algae and the garbage—and I felt myself give way to them.

Why did I think I could fix this?

Why was I so gosh darn certain that I had the answers?

I could be the one to stop this creature? To keep this park clean? To keep Frankie alive and well?

Who was I? I was no one. I was just a kid.

"Hey." Lyla's voice broke through my spiral. "Hey, Jean. Look at me."

And I did.

"We're gonna get through this."

And I listened to her. I drew in a shaky breath and shoveled another bit of sharp cheddar into my mouth.

"Yeah, you're right," I said finally. "We got this."

Byron came into the kitchen just as I took another bite of cheese.

"Frankie is gone," he blurted.

"Fuck," I said, "we don't got this."

There are so many noises. You prefer the quiet.

But one foot in front of the other, you walk toward them. Your legs are held upright by their bones, not the muscles you feel trembling.

The sun is hidden behind clouds. It is not yet night, but the sounds are like night.

Gripped in your left hand is an arm. Limp and wobbly.

You glance left. Another figure holds the other arm. The arms belong to someone familiar. But you can't quite put your mind on it long enough to focus.

Some of the sounds are coming from the body. It would be preferable to drop it.

You drag it the rest of the way.

Chapter 31

"Where did she go?" Lyla asked.

But I thought we all knew. "We have to hurry."

I grabbed the keys, and the three of us rushed out of the kitchen and piled into the pickup.

"Should we check on Meara and Sam?" Byron asked as we pulled out of my driveway. "I just called them, but neither picked up."

"If Frankie is gone, I'm willing to bet they are too." I put the truck into gear and flipped on the windshield wipers.

"Of course it's raining," Byron groaned as we turned out of the driveway and onto the street.

We were at the stop sign when Mojito came bounding into the middle of the road, stopping right in front of the truck, tail wagging, tongue out.

"This dog is everywhere," Lyla observed as Byron opened the door on his side and the dog hopped in. All seventy-five, sopping-wet pounds of doggo landed in Byron's lap, giving Lyla a giant lick on the cheek. "Guess she's invited?"

Based on how the water was clogged, I knew we needed to head to the far eastern side of the park. The paths were too narrow to get through the side neighborhood entrance, so I went to the parking lot side and to park as close to the path as I could get us.

On the short drive, Byron and Lyla tried to reach anyone they could but without any luck.

"You two don't have to come with me." I felt like it was a silly thing to say as soon as it came out of my mouth, but I'd faced this thing before and didn't want to put my friends in any more danger.

As I downshifted onto the gravel parking lot and put the truck into park, I caught withering looks from both of them out of the corner of my eye.

"Anyway." Byron's voice dripped with sarcasm. "Let's go fix this park."

Grateful that the leaves had not yet fallen and the rain made the ground soft and less crunchy, we worked our way as quickly and softly as we could toward the largest part of the waterways in the park.

The smell hit us before anything else.

Even with the wind blowing the opposite direction and the rain tamping down some of the air, it was overwhelming, and I had to stifle a cough. We pulled bandanas over our noses and, looking like Silver Dollar City train robbers, kept going.

The sounds were next. I knew the sloshing and slurping sound from before. I'd tried my best to describe it to Byron and Lyla, but by the way they both cringed, I knew I had done an imperfect job of it.

I led us through the woods to the spot where I'd rescued Sam, and it was definitely the right place. We crouched and half crawled to where we could see into the swamp.

Lyla squeezed my hand as we took in the sight.

Even though it was dark from the storm, we could see at least half a dozen kids from our school trapped and unconscious, wrapped in roots against the wall and partially submerged in the swamp mud, just their faces and hands poking out.

I bit my lip to keep from crying out when I recognized the two little skateboard kids.

With the rain pounding as it was, the stagnant water was rising and filling up quickly, getting closer to completely submerging some of the kids.

Then the ground where we crouched moved as if someone had stepped on top of a waterbed and we were on the other side of it. The grass and leaves buckled, and all of us wobbled where we bent down.

It's coming, I thought.

Lyla let out a gasp when the creature came into view, and I put my hand over her mouth.

It was even bigger than the first time I'd encountered it. It had to be.

Towering halfway as tall as the tallest trees, it was higher than a basketball goal, and lanky strings of weeds and algae covered its arms and body. Its head was an angry mass of mud and leaves and what looked like branches for horns. Its face was barely visible, save for glowing yellow-green eyes that shone through the foliage draping over its head. Long arms trailed all the way to the swamp floor like a robe of moss and grass.

It lumbered around the unconscious people who were trapped and unaware.

Across the water, Frankie stood with Meara, someone propped between them, and they walked toward the creature, letting the figure drop at its feet. Meara pushed it over with her boot so it lay face up.

It was frigging Jack again.

How many times was I going to have to rescue that guy?

The two of them stepped away, and with a wave of its limbs, the swamp thing had Jack wrapped around the arms and waist in vines, securing him to the murky grass. For the moment, the creature was not paying any attention to us.

And we needed to find a way to fix what we hoped was making it mad at all of us.

I elbowed Byron and nodded at them both to follow me, and we moved from our vantage point, crawling until we'd reached cover and the path. Then we picked up our tools and jogged to the small footbridge where it made the most sense that the blockage was occurring and causing the water to stagnate.

Sure enough, on the far east side, there was barely a trickly of water coming through where it should have been a flowing stream, especially during a rainstorm. The water on the other side was almost cresting the footbridge.

I lowered myself into the nearly empty pipe and walked the few feet to the grate. It was like looking at a solid wall of rock and mud and tree branches. The smallest trickle came through in a few small cracks, but it may as well have been cement. We had definitely found where all the debris from the sides of the creek had wound up. I climbed back out, taking Lyla's hand to get up to where she and Byron crouched.

So far, the thing still wasn't noticing us, but I knew lingering much longer was not an option.

"A bulldozer to this bridge would take care of it," Byron pointed out.

I agreed, but getting a bulldozer out here was not going to save the dozen kids that were currently trapped by the swamp monster. "We have to find a way to clear it from the other side."

Lyla took one hoe and raked at the opening. Byron and I took hold of the branches we could reach and pulled them up and out of the way.

It was slow though, and we needed to hurry.

Jumping into the water where Jack had disappeared, I took in a breath and dove, trying to feel around for where branches and other debris blocked the pipe, causing the stoppage and making the algae bloom worse. Caught against the grate was all manner of branches, and to my absolute dismay, I felt the blobby decay of what I was mentally prepared to assume was mud but was pretty sure was a mass of fish guts, or worse.

The water was completely stagnant as it pushed against the metal barriers that ran across both of the large pipes.

I came up retching.

Lyla reached down and pulled me out. "Are you okay?"

"Yeah, it's just really, really gross down there." And now I was wondering if I was up-to-date on my tetanus shot.

"We have to do something faster," Byron said, still pulling branches up, but they weren't making a difference.

"Do you think it hears us?" Lyla asked.

We still couldn't see the creature from where we were, but we could hear it around the bend where I'd rescued Blake and Sam the other night. And the noises were getting louder.

"If not, it's going to soon." I wiped the grime out of my eyes. "I have an idea on how we can speed things up. But we need to get to the truck right now."

We ran as quickly as we could back to the truck, jumped in and I explained my plan. "We'll have to wrap the straps around the biggest part of the blockage and use the truck to pull it out."

"Do you think that will work?" Byron asked.

"Only idea I have right now," I gritted my teeth and said a silent *please forgive me* to the park maintenance crew.

Then I slammed the truck into gear, bouncing over the railroad tie barriers that lined the parking lot, and rallied against my cringe as I drove the pickup down the widest gravel path in the park.

"When we get there, I'll wrap the straps around the tree trunk, and Byron, you can hook it to the truck?" I glanced at him and he gave me a thumbs up, looking a little green. These driving conditions were definitely not ideal.

The rain and wind were picking up too. Because of course.

I got to the foot bridge quickly though and had just enough room to get the truck lined up with the walkway.

Jumping out, we grabbed the ratchet straps we kept tucked behind the bench seat for anytime we needed to use the truck to transport, like, a refrigerator or other appliance for friends or family.

Which happened all the time if you had a truck. Like, on average every week.

I took one end and found the biggest log I could reach, running the strap underneath it and around one branch, while Byron secured the other end to the truck.

Once it was on tight, I jumped into the cab and floored it in reverse.

The branch moved, and all three of us let out a whoop of triumph. A loud creaking rang across the water as the branch loosened, and I angled the truck so that I could pull the branch onto the shore and out of the way.

Then the sound changed pitch, and a terrible crunching noise came from my truck as the front bumper ripped free.

I slammed on the emergency brake and screamed. An angry scream. A frustrated scream. A screw-you-universe scream.

"The bumper, Byron?" I got out and slammed the door, rushing over to undo the strap.

"Sorry." He grimaced and came to help me.

"Why would you attach it to the bumper?" I groaned.

"Y'all," Lyla called to us.

I looked up, the rain getting into my eyes, and swiped at them. "Yeah?" I called back.

"It definitely heard that." She pointed, and lumbering toward us was the Legend of Stonefish Creek.

You see the vines of the creature dragging along the ground in front of you.
See the mud-caked branches of its limbs.
Blood under your fingernails.
Four, the flash of a lightning strike.
Five, the glint of metal.

Four things you hear.
The grinding of tires against gravel.
Someone—your sister—calls your name.
A truck horn honks.
Tearing branches.

Three felt.
Rain against your cheeks, every drop.
Tiny rocks spinning though the air and peppering your cheeks and raised arms.
The smooth metal of a truck.

Smell of sewage, stagnant water.
Smell of fear.

Taste of copper floods your mouth. You've bitten your tongue or lost a tooth.
Grounded.
You wake up.

Chapter 32

The creature was coming toward us, Meara and Frankie flanking it on either side. There wasn't any time to waste, though now I was seriously questioning why we hadn't thought a few more things out a tad more thoroughly.

Looping the strap around the axel this time, Byron helped me knot it, and I jumped back into the water on the swamp side, while Lyla climbed into the open pipe on the other.

Holding my breath, I dove under and reached my hand as far back as I could past a large branch until I could feel the metal. I pushed the end of the strap through, hoped Lyla would be able to find it, and came back up for air.

"You got it?" I yelled.

Lyla responded quickly with a nod, Byron with a thumbs-up.

But we needed to loop the strap through, so I dove back in and felt around until I could find the other end, a few sections over from the first one I'd pushed through.

Yanking it through, we secured the other side in as good of a knot as we could, and I ran to get into the truck cab, wiping the rain from my eyes, feeling the mud smear over my face. We needed to unclog the pipe as quickly as we could to get the water moving.

The creature was lumbering toward us, dragging brush and weeds and trails of mud behind it. Instinct had me click on the seat belt as I slammed the truck into gear, grinding them in my rush. I pushed on the gas, but the tires just spun in the now muddier-than-before path.

We were going to have a lot of explaining to do about the state of these trails once this was all over.

I tried again, the truck swinging farther and farther side-to-side. The mud made it feel like it was sliding on ice.

The creature was close now. Almost in arms reach. Because it had some extremely long arms.

"Jean, get out of the truck!" Lyla yelled over the noise of the engine. I could see Byron waving frantically at me as well, telling me to get out. But we had to drain the creek.

I let off the gas and looked, not at the monster but at my sister, flanking it.

She tilted her head slightly then blinked, and through the pelting storm, I could see her rub her eyes, like she was waking up.

Then, like a lightbulb turning on, she was Frankie again.

She ran toward me, long, slender limbs navigating the mud like she was made for it.

Just as the monster reached the truck.

Its arms spread wide, flailing vines and branch-like limbs as long as a semi-truck. One slammed on the top of the pickup, denting the roof of the cab, and I barely had time to scream as a second one hit the passenger side so hard the mirror snapped off and the glass in the window shattered.

I had a brief moment to mourn both my bumper and mirror.

Then hands grabbed me from behind.

I shrieked and twisted around to see Frankie, standing in the bed of the truck, having flung open the back window.

"Jean, come on!" she yelled, pulling at me.

I unbuckled as a third arm smashed through the windshield, wrapping its way around the steering wheel and through the driver's side window where I had just been sitting.

As the creature took hold of the front tires and lifted the truck above the ground, Frankie helped me scramble out the back. She grabbed my hand and, over the roaring sound that was combination thunder and beast, yelled, "Jump."

And we did, landing with a crash on a muddy embankment, just as the creature swung the truck with such force it took out several trees and ripped the giant log we'd attached it to out of the ground in one giant slurping noise.

Water gushed through the opening it had made, a geyser forming on the other side for a few moments as the plug released the debris that had collected there.

Frankie stood up from where we'd landed and walked toward the swamp thing. The noises quieted and the rain turned to drizzle as she did.

I shakily followed her holding onto her elbow, "Frankie, no."

Mojito stood at the foot of the creature, tail wagging, tongue hanging lopsided from her mouth.

"Everyone freeze." Frankie dropped my arm where she was keeping me steady and held up her hands, fingers spread wide. "Shh."

"Frankie." I wiped the hair out of my face and did an internal assessment, but nothing seemed terribly out of place as far as organs and bones were concerned.

The creature stood hunched, its long vine arms trailing the ground and swinging gently. Mojito did a little spin and—Was the creature petting her? With its vine arms?

"Hey," Frankie said in soothing tones, walking slowly toward the creature, who seemed to notice only Mo.

In the no-longer-pounding rain, we could see the scene around us more clearly.

Mojito hopped away for a moment, and I held my breath as the creature swung its head around, tracking the dog's movements. But Mo came right back with a stick.

"What is happening?" Lyla asked. She was next to Byron, who stood beside me and Frankie.

I just shook my head.

"I think she wants it to throw the stick." Byron's jaw was in danger of becoming unhinged and not from all the tossing about we'd experienced a few minutes before.

Frankie shushed us again and took a few more steps toward the swamp thing.

"Frankie, don't," I started, but she shook her head.

"We can talk to it," she said and beckoned me forward with her gently.

"We can what to it?"

Frankie held out her hand to me and gave mine a squeeze. "Come on. I can help it know your intentions."

"I don't understand," I whispered.

"You don't have to. It's okay."

The creature used one vine on its body to scoop up the stick Mojito had chosen and then tossed it gently a few yards away. Mo bounded over, tail wagging the entire time, and brought it back.

I had to remember to take breaths as we walked within vine-arm-swinging distance and Frankie reached out and touched its arm.

Green and golden lights speckled up the creature from where her touch began, and it tilted its head, golden eyes glowing. The vines and arms that had so recently thrown my truck across the park—with us in it—were now humming with a soft moss green. As it looked between Frankie and me, it got smaller, little by little.

Frankie did not speak words out loud, but it looked like she was in a conversation with the creature. Frankie nodded toward me, and it bent its neck until it was looking me in the eye.

The orbs glowed softly, like a moon nightlight. It was unblinking. I wasn't sure it even had eyelids, but it paused, as though waiting for me to talk.

"Go ahead," Frankie encouraged.

"Go ahead and what?" I asked, trying not to shake.

Up close, the creature felt more like forest lichens or moss after a rain. It was shrinking, slowly bending closer to me. Also, having Mojito still running around as it threw sticks behind itself for her, unseeing as far as I could tell, but essentially the green light for *you can chill.*

"Just let it feel what you feel about Stonefish Creek," Frankie said. "It wants to understand." Frankie gently took one of the creature's vines and wrapped it loosely around my hand.

I took another breath and closed my eyes, focusing on how I felt about this place.

Its soft summers and crunchy ice patches in the winter. Fallen leaves collected in rainbow bouquets and pressed into dictionaries. Forts and trailing fingers in the water. Scooping up crawdads and letting them go. Keeping watch for the tadpoles until they hopped away as frogs.

A spring break playing *Lord of the Rings* running at full speed through the brush, seeing orcs out of the corner of our eyes. Crossing bridges as wide as Khazad-dum. High stakes. Low stakes. Fun stakes.

All the bruises and skinned knees. First kisses.

We'd seen a family of deer here once. Two females and two fawns. They were passing through, drinking from the spring. Frankie and I crouched behind the small boulder where we had been resting, watching the leaves against the blue sky.

At night, owls glided silently through the trees. Fish and turtles lined up on logs, jumping in when we crashed through the underbrush.

And cleaning up.

First out of habit, taking any trash we stumbled onto out of the park and into the bins. Then more construction, and we had more nails and roofing shingles. After windstorms, picking up garbage blown in by seventy-mile-an-hour straight winds, tossed here from upturned neighborhood cans.

Later, groups of students, clearing out the trash with more equipment and efficiency.

Frankie splashing me with creek water.

I opened my eyes. The creature was still peering at me. But it had shrunk to almost half its original size, and vines that had been taut and stretched out were loosely puddled at the bottom of the creature, pooled around where its feet would be.

Its eyes glowed softly, a gentle orange. No longer sharp or glaring. Just curious.

It raised one long vine and tapped me on the forehead. Warmth spread through my body, and I relaxed.

Then it turned and waded slowly into the creek, its vines and branches stretched below the surface of the water, and it sank a little at a time until it was submerged.

And then, finally, it was gone.

The noises of the park rushed back, and Mojito stood in front of us, stick in her mouth, tail still wagging.

Frankie squeezed my hand. "Come on, sis. We gotta dig those kids out. And Mojito needs a bath."

Chapter 33

Three weeks later, things were relatively back to normal. Though Frankie was overcompensating for freaking me out by checking in so often that I was becoming numb to worrying about her.

Was that a good thing? Had I grown?

Then it occurred to me that maybe it was on purpose so I'd ask her to stop and she could quit checking in all together.

All of us had been checking in on each other though. Once the creature had calmed down, the kids it had trapped woke up slowly and in various states of fogginess. I'd been in touch with the mom of one of the skateboard kiddos and it took them a few days, but they were back to normal according to her.

Kye, a representative from a corp group that had been cleaning up the devastation from the incident at Lake Hobotnica the previous summer, had volunteered to talk to the club about what we could do from here to make sure the riparian buffer—a fancy environmental term I was currently obsessed with and explained the harm from the erosion and why our swamp friend was so upset—was repaired and maintained.

They had been on a tour of the park with me, Blakely, and Frankie. Jack had resigned from his position as vice president, citing the irreparable bullshit he went through. Which, fair.

Kye helped us understand what was happening to the ecosystems in the park, why the erosion was a problem, and what options we had to fix it. The city council had threatened to close the park because of all the missing kids, but by the time they did an investigation, everyone either seemed to have forgotten what had happened or, in Jack's case, just lied and said they had.

I knew because he pulled me and Blakely aside and begged us to tell him he wasn't absolutely unhinged from reality. He remembered way more than even Sam, and I felt bad for him. Jack had become way more subdued. While not unwelcome, it was really weird.

"I think you all are going to be fine." Kye said. They had been showing us ways to track and measure the area between the water and solid ground so we could monitor the growth. We'd spent so much of our time as kids in that area. The part were it's soft and muddy but not too wet. Perfect for digging out little pools and catching crawdads.

"How long will repairing it take?" Frankie wore a beanie and waders that I'd insisted our moms help us buy.

Kye thought for a moment. "It really depends on a lot of factors like rain amounts and when the first freeze is. But there are some grants I can point you toward to help and even small changes can show a lot of improvements."

"Good, can't have any more swamp monsters snagging kids," Frankie said, and I nudged her and gave her a look.

"Swamp monster, huh?" Kye didn't even blink at the idea and just continued teaching us and pointing us toward other resources that could help, including the phone number of the man who ran a museum in Muskogee with no explanation other than "just in case."

After Kye left, Frankie and I headed home together, stopping by the spot where we'd seen the swamp creature last. We added a few branches we'd dragged over to the edge and gave the vines a little pat.

Explaining to my moms what had happened to my truck was basically impossible though. Every time we told them the truth, they just shook their heads. But they decided my punishment for wrecking it—absolutely not my fault—was that we didn't have a truck anymore and stopped at that.

Frankie and Meara had come back to the park several times at night and said they'd seen the swamp creature, but I hadn't gotten up the courage yet.

"You have to come with me tonight, Jean," Frankie insisted.

I had hesitated before, not wanting to risk reliving things, but after our talk with Kye and making a game plan with Blakely, I was feeling more confident.

"Okay, but I have to make sure Lyla is okay with it too." She and I had a date planned, and it was her turn to pick a movie for us to watch.

"Oh, I already talked to her. She's up for it." Frankie gave me a pat on the shoulder. "You shouldn't date my friends and expect me not to meddle."

"She wasn't your friend until we started dating though."

But Frankie wasn't having it. "I can't help it if everyone loves me."

She pulled me with her, and we went home to have dinner with our moms.

Once the sun set, Frankie, Meara, Lyla, and I met up and walked to the park. I had a flashlight but didn't need it since the moon was so bright. Lyla linked hands with me, and the shadows kept my blush from showing.

"Where are we going?" I asked, grateful that Frankie answered.

"Let's do the bridge today," Meara suggested, and she and Frankie led us to the tall bridge that crossed one of the creeks leading to the swamp. We all took seats, our feet dangling over the edge, chins resting on the metal bars. And waited.

And waited.

At some point, Lyla and I laid back and took turns pointing out constellations. It was unseasonably warm for November, not a surprise in Oklahoma, so the air was crisp and clear.

"Why do you think it targeted you?" I asked Frankie and Meara. We'd all been musing about this for the past few weeks. Nothing concrete had come from it, but we all had theories.

Meara shrugged. "Your guess is as good as mine."

"I have thoughts about it," Frankie said.

I waited for her to elaborate, but she didn't offer anything else.

Then Meara whispered, "It's here."

We sat up and looked across the water. The creature, much smaller than before, drifted softly across the swamp, arms trailing gently, causing ripples in the water. It cast a soft glow, and several softly glowing orbs floated around it, sometimes dipping gently into the water, the reflections casting delicate shapes under the surface.

My breath caught as it waved one of its arms.

Vines grew magically fast from the appendage, wrapping themselves along one edge of the creek, doing exactly the type of repairs we had been learning about that afternoon. Its glow pulsed and then faded as the vines attached themselves to the buffer, and it disconnected, moving slowly back the way it had come, until it was no more than a shadow to us.

"We got this." I gave Lyla's hand a squeeze and leaned my head on Frankie's shoulder.

Acknowledgements

Well well well, acknowledgements section, we meet again. Firstly, I wrote this book for a dog named Frankie who is a shop dog at Ranch Acres and let me pet her one time and also another two times sniffed my leg enough that I felt her little nose. And because I'm a totally logical person I decided to name a main character after her in the hopes that it would convince her to let me pet her for a frequent and possibly extended period of time.

ANYWAY shop local and women owned, bonus points if they have shop dogs.

To my Oma who told me countless stories, made wonderful nature scavenger hunts, and instilled in me a love of art and travel and a healthy fear of drowning.

Thank you Marshall, for everything. But especially this time because our everything has kind of ballooned in a good way and I appreciate you more than ever. Hopefully you'll read this one since I basically based all of the wishy washy science off the research the dude you worked for did. I love you so dearly.

Also to G because you left me alone just long enough to finish it and someday when you're creating, I'll do my best to leave you alone just long enough to finish what you're doing.

Meredith, you brought the best dog in the world into my life and this story, while a swamp monster one, is mostly about a really good dog named Mojito. Based on the really best dog named Arizona. I love you so much and I also love Rocket and Fable and Knightly…but I mean come on.

To Tina, my long lost bestie, to Nicole at Positive Space for creating such a lovely space, to Alice and the other twitch co-workers who keep me motivated, to the B2Weirdos who are my OG dedication now and always. To Jeni who continues to be a powerhouse in my life, Sandy who keeps her shit in line, and Whitney who brought us together.

To the siblings, cousins and friends who ran around Ray Harrell Nature Park with me for countless hours while we grew up and especially while we refused to grow up. And to my mom and dad for encouraging us to run around out there.

To Chuck, and Kye, and Dani, and Jean, and Geraldine who are letting me tell their stories.

And to all the queer okies, old and young and just thinking about things, who want to see themselves in adventures and have a good time with their noses in a book. I see you. I am you. And I love you.

About the Author

Jes lives in Tulsa, Oklahoma with her partner and their kiddo. As well as two weenie dogs, Rocket Xavier and Fable Rose Pond. When she's not writing, she is working at a community arts center in her hometown and making art. She loves board games, soft sci-fi and pirate shows, and using stickers in her planner.

Jes is primarily a Science-Fiction, Fantasy, and Horror YA author whose works are full of ensemble disaster queer casts and the occasional crime and/or alien. She writes books that are nostalgic and humorous with (spoiler alert) happy endings for the sweet baby gays. (An editor once compared her writing to "Stranger Things minus the trauma").

Her debut novel "Chronicles of My Alien Invasion Life" came out Summer 2022, followed by "A Mean Piece of Water" in December of 2022.

In addition to novels, she is also a poet and editor. She edited and contributed poems and photography to "Between the Mess and Magic", a collaborative parenting poetry collection. She co-founded Horns And Rattles Press, an indie press located in Tulsa. Their first anthology "Fish Gather to Listen" came out summer 2023, and their second anthology "Bitter Become the Fields" summer 2024.

To contact, email Jes at *jesmccutchen@gmail.com*